CW00666238

Reluctantly Rescued

The Barrington Billionaires

Book Nine

Ruth Cardello

Author Contact

website: RuthCardello.com
email: ruthcardello@gmail.com
Facebook: Author Ruth Cardello
Twitter: RuthieCardello
Goodreads
goodreads.com/author/show/4820876.Ruth_Cardello
Bookbub
bookbub.com/authors/ruth-cardello

New York Times and *USA Today* bestselling author Ruth Cardello returns with a hilarious addition to the Barrington Billionaire series.

Copyright

Print Edition

ISBN eBook: 978-1-951888-05-3
ISBN Print: 978-1-951888-06-0

An original work of Ruth Cardello, 2020.

Dedication

This book is dedicated to Serenity.

Thank you for helping me plot out the fight scene. You rock!

Chapter One

"Isn't he something?" a woman beside Bradford Wilson asked as he hauled his jean-clad ass out of a pond in Oklahoma. Her voice was wistful and her eyes full of admiration but not for Bradford.

"Yeah, something," he said in a mocking tone she didn't seem to notice. He was soaking wet from the waist down. She was dressed in flat sandals and a yellow flowered sundress that flattered her curvy figure. Pretty in a girl-next-door kind of way. Light makeup, bright smile, she exuded a sweet innocence he had no interest in. Still, it irked him that she was holding a towel for a man who appeared to be in no rush to get out of the water while not acknowledging the dripping wet man beside her.

"Wasn't it amazing when he caught those two fish with his bare hands?"

"Amazing." Noodling was a "sport" Bradford had only recently become aware of. Leave it to Connor to propose at an event where everyone was using their bare hands as fish bait. Bradford didn't have patience for many people, but he made time for Connor because he was fucking hilarious even when he wasn't trying to be.

Bradford would have flown out for the proposal for that reason alone, but he'd also been asked by Ian Barrington to secure the area for the event. The Barringtons didn't go anywhere blind.

When Bradford looked around he saw the crowd in terms of what he'd discovered about them via a background check: type of employment, marital status, known substance abuse, registered weapons, as well as any criminal history. The locals were harmless. Connor had chosen a woman with a good crew. Almost too good to believe.

Like the woman beside Bradford, Joanna Ervin was one of Angelina's friends from New Jersey. He'd done a more thorough background check on her than anyone else there because it bothered him when he couldn't find anything wrong with a person.

Born and raised on a small horse farm in western New Jersey, she'd never gotten so much as a speeding ticket. Although she'd moved closer to New York for college, she was still well liked in her hometown. In her high school yearbook she'd been listed as "Most likely to make you smile."

Her last relationship had ended amicably after a year. That didn't seem right. Who calls it off after a year with no ill feelings? Bradford had made it a point to not only meet the guy she'd dated, but also get him drunk enough to answer some pretty personal questions.

He'd had only good things to say about Joanna—said he would have married her, but somehow, over time, he'd slid into the friend category.

Bradford glanced at the beautiful woman beside him. Friends after a year? *One or both of them must have been bad fucks.*

Her bright smile confirmed that she was no mind reader. He didn't smile back. Her gaze wandered downward. She blinked a few times quickly, then asked, "Did you bring swim trunks?"

"Would I be standing here in wet jeans if I had?"

Her eyebrows rose and fell, then she shrugged. "I didn't bring a suit either. Call me a bleeding heart, but I feel bad for the catfish. They're only defending their nests."

"They're fucking fish." He frowned and looked away as soon as he'd said it. He filtered himself around most people, but there was something about her that made stupid shit come out of his mouth. "Wait, let me guess, you're a vegetarian."

She didn't look bothered by his growled accusation. "I am, but if you're looking to fight about it, you'll be disappointed. I live my life and let others live theirs."

"That works until you meet an asshole."

She laughed and wagged a finger. "Good point."

He hadn't said it as a joke. He didn't like that nothing seemed to bother her. *Not even me.* People shied away from him normally. Crowds parted for him. The hands of armed men shook when he stared them down. Even the US government wasn't sure they could control him.

Some say a person's eyes are a window to their soul. Bradford had been told his were cold and dark. Not shocking—a piece of him died with every life he took, and he'd taken more than any man should.

Her attention had returned to Dylan Sutton. "I can't get over how much he looks like Connor. If I married him and we had children they might look just like Connor and Angelina's. How adorable would that be?"

Marry? What the fuck was she talking about? "You're interested in Dylan?"

Joanna hugged the towel to her chest and a dreamy look entered her eyes. "Crazy right? I'm not saying anything will happen, just letting myself dream. I wish I'd met him before he became a movie star. How could I compete with the beautiful women who are falling all over him now?"

Bradford had had enough of the conversation. He was about to walk away when Joanna grabbed his arm.

"Here he comes. Quick, look like I just said something funny."

He pulled away from her touch. He didn't like how it had sent warmth through him nor that the smile she was flashing him was for the benefit of another man.

When Dylan walked by without glancing at her, she pursed her lips. "He didn't even notice me this time."

"You can do better than that idiot."

She laid a hand on his arm again as if his reaction to her initial touch hadn't been negative. "He's not an idiot. On the surface he and Connor act like big lugs, but they have hearts of gold. Look at how good Connor is with Angelina's son—you'd think they'd known each other all their lives. I know you can't hurry love, but when I see Angelina and

Connor together it gives me happy goose bumps." She hugged the towel to her chest. "It might sound like a foolish dream, but I want the fairy tale."

He stared back at her, not saying a word. Dylan and Connor weren't the problem; his reaction to this sparkly, upbeat woman was. As she looked up at him, his heart began to thud. They could not be more different. She was the type who probably "relocated" spiders outside because every life was precious. When he took aim, it was for a kill shot. She was dreaming of living happily ever after. The best he hoped for was to die doing something important.

Her gaze dipped down his chest and lower. Her cheeks were pink when her eyes met his again. "Would you like the towel?"

He shook his head. Dylan wasn't a bad guy. She could do much worse. Still, he didn't like the image of her with him, gathering with the Barringtons, raising a litter of optimistic, beautiful children.

Am I so fucking miserable I can't stand the idea of anyone being happy?

She leaned closer and his breath caught in his throat. Her voice was like warm honey, sweet and addictive. "Hey, don't tell anyone what I said about marrying Dylan, okay? My friends already think I'm a flake when it comes to dating."

He could have told her he wouldn't, but instead he just held her gaze. He found the less he said the better it was for everyone. He gave her a look that usually had people taking a step back from him.

She continued, "If it doesn't work out, that's fine, but a

girl has to try, right?"

Why won't she shut up? What does she want from me? He decided to toss her a bone. "Don't look so eager."

Her forehead furrowed. "Excuse me?"

Bradford groaned. "Don't wait for him on the beach with a towel. If you want him to notice you, stop trying to get his attention."

She nodded and glanced down at the towel. "You're so right. I'm playing this all wrong." Her smile returned. "Thanks, Bradford."

Warmth spread up his neck at the sound of his name on her lips. He frowned and tried to recall the face of the last woman he'd been with—less than a week ago, the one who had gone down on him on the drive back to her place. She'd been talented then and in bed later. Why was he having such a hard time recalling her face?

Joanna tapped a finger to her chin. "I've never been good at playing hard to get, but maybe that's why I'm still single. This isn't just any guy—this is Dylan Sutton. If things worked out between us I could actually be related to my best friend. We could raise our babies together. That alone should be enough incentive for me to up my game."

When Bradford didn't answer, Joanna looked around for Dylan. He was standing next to his father within a circle of locals who were asking for his autograph. "Do you think he's out of my league?"

Bradford gave Joanna a slow once-over and made a pained sound deep in his chest. She was neither flirting with him nor digging for a compliment. Did she genuinely not know how fucking good-looking she was?

Without waiting for him to respond, she squared her shoulders and said, "There I go doubting myself again. No one is out of anyone's league, right? People are just people. I have to stop trying so hard. All I can do is put myself in the right place at the right time, and if magic is meant to happen it will." Her smile did crazy things to Bradford's ability to think straight. "You're easy to talk to, Bradford. Thank you."

With that, Bradford did the only thing that seemed to make sense to do—he turned on his heel and walked away.

SOON AFTER BRADFORD'S departure, Joanna's friend Aly appeared at her side. She said, "Connor's proposal will forever stand out as the most unique I've ever seen. How about you?"

"Definitely. I loved when he acted like the fish was too big for him to catch so he suggested she try it. And she did it and found the ring instead. I would have never guessed she grew up in a place like this. He brings out a side of her I had no idea existed."

"That's for sure. And it's a good one."

Joanna smiled in the direction of the couple. "He stands taller when she's around. She obviously makes him happy. I love it."

Aly nodded in agreement. "Me too."

Even though Aly was one of Joanna's closest friends, she was not above mocking Joanna's desire to find a Prince Charming and settle down. Some people had huge dreams of making the world a better place. Aly was doing her share via her inventions in the female diagnostics field. Joanna's dreams had always been much smaller, much closer to home.

She'd grown up as the only child of two loving parents and adoring grandparents. She had cousins who regularly asked her when she planned to move back home and settle down. She had old friends who asked the same.

Her life wasn't perfect, but she kept her focus on the good in it. Family. Friends. Her new career as an author of a top-selling children's book series about her rescue miniature horse, Betty. She was not only able to make a living off her new income, but also support the rescue and rehabilitation of other minis.

The only thing missing? Someone to share her life with. Her biological clock was ticking. Marriage wasn't for everyone, but she couldn't imagine herself without a husband and child.

"I saw you talking to Dylan earlier. How'd that go?" Aly asked.

Joanna shrugged. "He seemed nice."

"He's gorgeous. Most people don't live up to their on-screen presence, but he absolutely does. Very sexy. Are you interested in him?"

"Why? Are you?"

"Not if you are." Oh, crap. It was one thing to be competing with nameless swarms of bikini-clad fans, but she and Aly had never set their sights on the same man. "I do think he's hot, but if you tell me you're interested, I'm not that into him."

"I feel the same way. If you want him, just say so. No big

deal."

For some reason that tickled Joanna's sense of humor. "Is it that easy? We toss a coin and the winner gets him? I admire your confidence."

Aly laughed. "You know what I meant. Our friendship means a lot more to me than any man ever will."

A little devil in Joanna wanted to test that claim. "Okay, then I'll take him."

Aly's eyes narrowed slightly, then she smiled. "Whew, that's a weight off my shoulders. I was thinking buying a condom in this town is probably equivalent to taking out a billboard sign announcing you're engaging in intercourse."

Joanna shook her head. When it came to books, Aly was a hundred, possibly a thousand times smarter than she was. Aly'd gotten her PhD while Joanna was still working on her bachelor's degree. But when it came to people? Men in particular? Aly was lost. She very rarely dated because, by her own admission, she lacked whatever romance gene was required for it.

Given a real shot at Dylan, Aly probably would have sex with him once or twice then decide it couldn't work out— for whatever reason she came up with that day—and it would be over. So, by claiming Dylan for herself, Joanna was actually doing their circle of friends a favor. Awkward breakups could add a strain to even strong friendships, and Aly and Angelina were like sisters to her.

Still, Joanna felt she needed to clarify their stance one last time. "Seriously, though, if you like him I would never go after a man you felt something for."

"I know that," Aly said then hugged Joanna. "The world is full of beautiful, rich men. You can have this one."

Relief washed over Joanna and a level of giddiness returned. "He's just so perfect. Do you know he does all his own stunts? Angelina said he's humble too, like Connor. He has the same goofy sense of humor." She grimaced. "Can you imagine us together?"

Without missing a beat, Aly said, "Absolutely. You've got a wholesome vibe a man like him would be drawn to. Just be careful."

"Oh, I intend to be. I'm going to play it cool—let him chase me."

"That's smart." She cleared her throat. "Speaking of being careful. I wouldn't get too close to Bradford."

"Why not?" Joanna straightened in surprise and searched the crowd for him. He was standing beside Ian Barrington, looking more like a bodyguard than the friend everyone said he was. When their eyes met, Joanna waved. He didn't wave back.

She wasn't offended because she doubted his lack of response had anything to do with her. Like a brokenhearted horse sold to a kill lot, someone had taught him to avoid a kind hand. As with the animals she worked with, she understood patience and consistency was the key to earning his trust. She smiled at him and thought, *It's okay, Bradford. You take your time. When you're ready you'll see I'm not so bad.*

"Look at him."

Joanna frowned and turned back to face her friend. "Since when do you judge someone by how they look? Every one of his tattoos might be a tribute to someone he loves. He might have gotten those scars while saving people. We don't know what he does."

"Exactly, we don't know, and I wasn't referring to his scars or tattoos. I've never seen him unarmed. Today he doesn't appear to have a gun, but my guess is he has a weapon somewhere on him. They say he's Ian's friend, but that's not his role here."

"You think he's their security detail?"

"He's more than that. He's dangerous, Joanna. Just promise me you'll be careful around him."

Joanna looked across the crowd and found Bradford still watching them. "He wouldn't be here if he was some horrible person. Angelina approves of him. I don't get a bad vibe from him at all. You're being paranoid."

"I don't think so. His last name is Wilson. Guess what happens when you look Bradford Wilson up online?"

"What?"

"You find nothing."

"Isn't that a good thing?"

"No social media? No mention in any of the articles about the Barringtons? I couldn't find a single photo of him online."

"So he's a private person. That's actually refreshing. Some people post too much."

"I wonder if Wilson is even his last name."

"I wonder if the birthmark on my left arm could have been left during an alien abduction I don't remember, but then I yank myself back to reality. Does anyone here look afraid of Bradford?"

Aly pressed her lips together, then admitted, "No."

"And they've known him a lot longer. Angelina said he and Ian have been friends for over a decade. So stop judging his book by his cover. You're more open-minded than that, Aly."

Aly sighed. "I am. I'm sorry. It's just something I see in his eyes that makes the hair on the back of my neck stand up."

Joanna looked over at Bradford again. He did have a certain look in his eyes, but it was one that pulled on her heartstrings. "Someone hurt him, Aly. He needs your understanding, not your judgement. Give him a chance. He just might surprise you."

Out of her peripheral vision Joanna saw Dylan walk by. He didn't stop but he did nod and smile at them.

Joanna brought a hand to her mouth. "Did you see that? He smiled at us."

"Oh, boy. If you like him that much, go talk to him."

"No, I'm doing this the right way. If he wants to talk to me, he'll have to come over here."

"He's hitting on that woman in the cut-off shorts."

"That's okay. She can be his tonight, I'll be his forever," Joanna said with confidence. She linked her arm with Aly's. "Come on. Enough talk about men, let's go find Angelina. This is her day."

Chapter Two

A MONTH LATER Bradford stood in the shadows of a large ballroom that would soon be packed with Boston's rich and famous. Although he hadn't been asked to, he'd walked the hired security company through a list of scenarios they needed to prepare for.

Ian Barrington entered the room, spotted him, and headed over. "I knew you'd be here."

Bradford didn't acknowledge his comment. He didn't have to. They'd known each other long enough that Ian didn't expect a response.

Moving to stand beside him, Ian said, "We hired top-notch security for the event. You can relax."

"The world hasn't become a safer place, Ian, you've just become soft."

"If by soft you mean I'm no longer willing to risk my hide on a regular basis, I concede that I have. Marrying Claire changed my priorities. I can make a difference without dodging bullets."

Bradford folded his arms across his chest. In their early twenties, while Bradford was still in the service, forty young girls had been abducted in a Third World country—straight out of their school. Bradford was Special Ops serving in the area as part of an off-the-record reprimand for insubordination. He'd defied a direct order he hadn't agreed with because it had involved injuring innocent civilians. The rebel leader who decided to take those girls for his men had chosen the wrong time and place to do it. Only a few towns away, Bradford had requested leave to help retrieve the girls. When his request was denied, he'd sent a brief text to his superior telling him where he was going and exactly what he could do with his refusal.

Ian had also been moved by the girls' plight and had arrived with a team of young, inexperienced hired soldiers. Unaware of each other, Bradford and Ian attempted to free the girls on the same night. Ian lost half his team. Bradford had gotten stabbed. Together, though, they'd freed the schoolgirls and returned them to their families.

Ian would have stopped there, but Bradford couldn't. He'd hunted down the ringleaders of that kidnapping and took them out, one by one. The rebels who remained understood they could challenge their government, but death would come if they crossed the line and harmed innocents again.

Bradford had expected to be court-martialed, but instead he received an education on the power and influence money wielded. Ian had the kind of friends who played presidents like puppets. The whole story stayed out of the news and Bradford received an honorable discharge. In his own way, Ian had saved Bradford's life, and that was a strong foundation for a friendship.

Over the next ten years, the two of them were offered countless missions by the US government, but took only the ones that fit their moral code. They worked under the radar, outside the normal chain of command—both willing to give their lives to protect civilians.

Until Ian met Claire and fell in love. When Claire had asked Bradford to help Ian land a job running a top-secret foreign relations department of the CIA, Bradford hadn't imagined Ian would actually take a desk job. It had sounded like another cover story, one that would allow Ian to continue his old ways without detection.

To Bradford's surprise, Ian had meant what he'd said about backing away from the front lines. Unaware that Bradford had gotten him the job, Ian had negotiated for Bradford to co-head the department with him. Unlike Ian, though, Bradford had nothing he was afraid of losing.

With that in mind, Bradford asked, "How is Claire?"

"Great. We're trying to start a family. Sounds easy, but with Claire it involves charts and graphs. I had no idea so much thought went into what some people come to by accident."

"That's what you get when you marry a life coach."

Ian smiled. "I don't mind. I've never been happier." Bradford believed him. Claire was a good match for him—poised and sophisticated on the surface, strong and full of grit when she needed to be.

They stood in comfortable silence for a few minutes, then Ian said, "Thank you for coming today. It was important to my mother."

He nodded once in acknowledgement of Ian's show of gratitude, then said, "I was in the area." He hadn't been, but it wasn't something he'd admit.

Ian clapped a hand on Bradford's shoulder. "Well, I'm glad you're here. I should have brought you home to meet my parents years ago, but now you get to experience why I didn't. They don't understand boundaries. You're one of us now, which means if I have to suffer through charity events, you do as well."

Bradford didn't voice his gut response to Ian's words. He was far from being "one of them." Sophie and Dale Barrington were good people, which meant Bradford didn't mind going out of his way for them, but that was as far as it went. Over the past decade, Ian and Bradford had had each other's backs. They had an unspoken loyalty to watch out for each other and, because of that, Ian was the closest thing Bradford had to family. That feeling didn't extend, however, to the rest of the Barringtons.

Asher was a pompous ass. If his wife was around, he was tolerable, but Bradford could stomach him for about a heartbeat before he wanted to smash his face in.

Grant was a financial genius but required frequent reminding as far as what was and was not his business. Ian claimed Grant asked questions because he wanted to help, but Bradford didn't need anyone's help in the financial department. He was already set for life. Grant's wife, Viviana, was definitely his better half—especially since she brought with her the comic relief of Connor and Dylan

Sutton, two meatheads who marched to their own tune even as they tried to fit in with the Barringtons.

Lance—okay, there was nothing to not like about Lance. He'd married a soft-spoken woman and seemed to spend most of his days chasing their twin daughters around and looking happy to do it. Was it possible for someone to be too nice?

Kenzi was sweet, but she'd married Dax Marshall who was another arrogant prick with the added negative bonus of being close friends with Clay Landon—a royal pain in the ass on his best day. The first time they'd met, Dax had taken Bradford aside and thanked him for watching out for Ian.

As if I'd done it for him.

Sure—you're welcome. Now back the fuck up.

Perhaps because Kade had been raised away from the family, he was the most likeable of the bunch. He and his wife went back and forth between Boston and Australia, straddling the lives they had in each country. He didn't ask questions, didn't look for trouble. To Bradford, he was a man who was just grateful to have survived the fallout of discovering the woman who'd raised him was not his real mother.

All things considered, it wasn't a surprise that the Barringtons were all fucked in the head. Still, Bradford didn't consider any of that his business. He boxed up any feelings he had about Ian's family, stuffed them deep in his gut and kept his interactions with them superficial. They didn't matter. They were part of his life, but would they always be? Probably not.

"How long are you in town?" Ian asked.

Bradford shrugged. He had a few things in the works, but nothing urgent.

"The family is gathering at my parents' tomorrow night. You're welcome to join us."

"Hard no."

Ian sighed. "The invitation is always there. I didn't see the lure of game night at first, but I have to admit it's nice to see everyone in that atmosphere. The games let us gather and have something to talk about that isn't serious. It's also amazing to see how fast my nephews and nieces are growing up."

Bradford shot Ian a look and hoped it expressed how he felt.

Ian laughed. "Okay, so none of that tempts you yet. Someday it might. Who knows, you might find someone who makes you consider a desk job as well."

"Never. Going. To. Happen."

Ian checked his phone after it beeped. "Claire will be here, but she's also working the event. One of her clients is terrified of crowds so Claire had my mother invite her."

"Sounds like my cue to leave."

"You can't, everyone is looking forward to seeing you. Sneak out before my mother sees you, and you know she will hunt you down."

Sophie would too. Bradford growled deep in his chest.

"Don't worry, Mom put you at the fun table: Dylan, Connor, Angelina, Aly, Joanna, Clay, and Lexi. You might end up with Claire's client as well. Two single men, two, maybe three, single women. How bad could it be? Aly's a doctor, she might be able to help you with whatever has been stuck up your ass lately."

When Bradford didn't say anything, Ian added, "Unless you think Dylan is too much competition for you. Movie star. Pretty-boy face. I get why you'd be intimidated."

"Shut the fuck up."

"Keep an open mind. You're not bad-looking when you smile."

Bradford was about to say something cutting when Joanna entered the room in an off-the-shoulder, floor-length emerald gown. Her hair was swept up in a loose knot, revealing a long and oh-so-tempting neck. The front of her gown was tight, pushing the swell of her breasts above it. It was enough to leave Bradford temporarily unable to speak.

Ian followed his gaze. "Oh, good, Joanna's here. Claire asked her to come early so her client wouldn't feel alone when she arrives."

Joanna looked around the still mostly empty room then smiled when she spotted Bradford and Ian. She waved.

Bradford raised his hand ever so slightly in response before tensing as he realized she was walking over to greet them. He'd had a month to tell himself she was nothing special, a month to forget how just a look from her set his heart racing.

She greeted Ian with a hug and a smile, then turned to Bradford. "I'm a hugger, but you can tell me no."

"No," he said in a guttural tone.

Her smile widened and she held out her hand. "Then,

Mr. Wilson, it's a pleasure to see you again."

He closed his hand around hers, realizing only after he'd done it what a mistake even that was. Her grip was strong, her skin rough from working on her small farm. Despite the innocence of their connection, his mind flooded with images of her running her hands all over his body. Never had he felt so close to kissing a woman he had absolutely no intention of doing anything with. He dropped her hand. "Joanna."

She leaned in. "The Mr. Wilson thing was a joke. You were supposed to laugh."

He gave her the same cold look that tended to shut most people down. In his experience silence was a formidable defense. Assholes looked for easier targets, nice people felt awkward and moved on as well.

She didn't do either. Instead she gave his arm a pat. "Don't worry, I know you missed me."

Ian gave them both a long look then excused himself and walked away.

As soon as they were alone again, Joanna said, "Bradford, you have no idea how glad I am you're here. When Claire told me I'd be sitting at the same table as Dylan tonight, I started to way overthink this. On one hand, sure it'll give me a chance to talk to him, but on the other hand what if he thinks I arranged to be seated with him? I haven't seen him since Oklahoma and I played it cool there. Maybe too cool—he hooked up with a local woman. Angelina said he hasn't mentioned her since so—I don't know."

I always knew I was destined for hell. I earned my time there, but I had no idea my sentence would begin while I was still breathing.

She looked around the room. "Oh, good, the bar is open. I need a boost of confidence. I can't drink alone. Join me?"

"Sure," he said. Maybe a stiff drink would help his hardening cock realize she was not interested in him.

She slid her arm through his, a move that caused his forearm to graze across the side of her breast. He sucked in a breath then told himself to calm the fuck down. If she noticed at all, she gave no indication of it. "So, what have you been up to since I last saw you?"

He swallowed hard. "This and that." It wasn't as if he could tell her about the sniper shot to the middle of the forehead he'd given the man who'd abducted a congressman's daughter. Neither the abduction nor the rescue would ever make the news or be tied to his name, and that was how it needed to remain.

"What do you do?" she asked.

He didn't answer.

She paused and looked up at him. "You don't have to tell me if you don't want to. Do you like it, though? Whatever it is that you do?"

A man could get lost in eyes like hers—so open, so trusting. "I find parts of it fulfilling."

She nodded then started walking again. "I get that. I went through a lot of jobs before I found one I could say truly fit me. I never imagined myself as an author of children's books, but it has been a game changer for me. I finally have the cash flow to do the things I used to think only other people could do."

He needed to know. "Such as?"

"Ever since I rescued Betty, I've always wanted to help more miniature horses, but finding them the perfect home is difficult. However, since my books have done so well I've been able to afford to bring in incredible trainers. I'm excited to be able to say that we are now an official pre-training facility for service and seeing-eye horses."

Was that even a thing? "Sounds—interesting."

"Try fascinating, rewarding, life-changing good. Imagine seeing a throw-away miniature horse at an auction or in a kill pen. Society has decided it has little to no value. But that's far from the truth. They have so much to give. With the right training, that little horse can open a blind child's life. It can be a support animal for people of all ages. It's the kind of work that makes every day a good one. I still pinch myself; now and then when I start to wonder if this is really my life."

She was too happy, and it made him angry although he couldn't pinpoint why. "When you buy anything from a kill pen you're supporting the kill lot business."

Her lips pursed. "I've heard that argument, but you know who doesn't care about that? The minis I rescue. No matter what you do in life, someone will say it's wrong. All I can do is follow my heart and have faith that I'm saving the ones that are meant to be saved."

"Faith," he snorted. "The perfect sand to bury your head in."

She turned toward him again. "You don't have to believe in what I do, but do you believe in something?"

He could have lied, but as he looked down into her eyes

he didn't want to. "I believe we only get one ride, so we'd better make it count for something."

She touched his arm. "That's beautiful."

He jerked away, breaking the connection almost immediately. He was torn between warning her to never touch him again or hauling her up over his shoulder and carrying her off to somewhere she could touch him as much as she liked.

"This dress is being difficult. I'm more the T-shirt and jeans kind of girl." She wiggled and adjusted the top of her dress. Then as if she hadn't just pushed her breasts upward and given him a perfect view of a brain-scrambling amount of cleavage, she asked, "How about I buy the first drink?"

"It's an open bar." He refused to think about how much he'd like to help her out of that dress, refused to let his thoughts wander to where drinking together might lead them.

"Of course it is. I should know that." She blushed. "I suppose I'll have to learn things like that if I intend to marry into the family, right?"

She'd said it as if she were joking, but it didn't ring funny to Bradford. "What do you want to drink?" Even though people were arriving and there were others at the bar, the bartender nodded at Bradford immediately. Bradford lowered his head so he could hear Joanna's response.

"I should say wine," she said tentatively.

"You should say what you want."

"I may look calm on the outside, but on the inside I'm a bundle of nerves. Let's get something stronger."

"A shot of tequila it is." He expected her to refuse, but she nodded almost as if in relief. No one he'd spoken to about her had mentioned that she was a drinker. "On one condition."

"And that is?"

"We do it right."

"Salt on the hand? Lime at the end?"

"There's a better way."

"I'm game to learn." Her lips curled in a sweet smile that was so tempting he almost kissed her. He straightened and ordered the tequila extra añejo with salted lime wedges. The bartender held up a bottle of a top-label brand. Bradford nodded once in acceptance.

He handed her a glass and a slice of lime then accepted his from the bartender.

He held his shot up. She mirrored his stance. "What's the first thing you notice?" he asked.

She studied her drink. "It's golden rather than clear."

"Exactly. The clear tequila, blanco, is essentially straight out of the vat, which is why it's harsh on the throat. This one has spent a decade or more in red wine barrels before being finished in American oak barrels. It's sweet with just enough spice to keep it interesting." A lot like the woman smiling up at him. "For that reason, it should be sipped, not gulped."

"So, we're not just tossing this back then biting into the lime. Got it." She sniffed the liquor. "I'm trusting you, Bradford. Don't do me wrong."

He considered telling her she shouldn't trust him—no one should. He'd lost whatever was good in him a long time ago. Instead he raised his glass higher. "Just a sip."

She hesitated. "Do I bite into the lime before? After?"

"Neither. Not the first time."

Joanna made a face in anticipation of not liking it, but she closed her eyes and did as he'd suggested. Her eyes flew open. "Oh, that's not bad. You're right, it's smooth."

"All the pleasure without the pain. Isn't everything better that way?" He hadn't intended to go there, but she was messing with his ability to think straight.

She searched his face. "Yes." Her voice was husky and intoxicating. He was a man who was always hyper-aware of his surroundings. In his line of work people didn't last long if they lowered their guard.

He could normally list not only all the people present and their location in the room, but also what they were wearing and if they had anything in their hands. There could have been a man swinging a machete beside Bradford in that moment and he wouldn't have noticed.

Cheeks flushed, she looked away. "So what do we do with the lime?"

He knew he was entering dangerous waters. Desire didn't necessitate action. He wasn't an adolescent learning to control himself. Joanna was a nice woman who may or may not realize she was turning him on. Either way it would be a mistake to get involved with her. She was too innocent. Too trusting. The corner of his mouth twisted wryly as he imagined how fast she'd run from him if she knew even a sliver of what he'd done.

Still, he raised his lime wedge. "This time squeeze a little of your salted lime into your mouth then take a sip."

Their gaze met and held. She raised her slice in perfect timing with him. They squeezed, sipped, swallowed in unison.

His brain completely shut down as he fought back an impulse to lick the salt off her lips. He downed the rest of the shot and slapped it back onto the bar.

She copied him, returning her glass as well. They stood there for a moment, not speaking, not looking at each other.

A movement at the door of the ballroom caught his eye. He growled, "Your friend is here."

Joanna expelled an audible breath. "Oh, good. And she's with Daphne. Claire asked us to help her feel comfortable here." She waved them over.

The appearance of her friends created an easy out for him. "I should—"

She touched his forearm. "Stay. We're all at the same table. This is your chance to get to know them."

Bradford looked down at her hand on his arm then raised his eyes to hers. He didn't pull away this time. His heart was beating wildly in his chest and he couldn't get his feet to move.

"Please." Joanna shot a persuasive smile at Bradford and warmth spread through him as he caved to her charm.

"Sure."

JOANNA HAD NEVER been into the "bad boy" type, but she had to admit she had a growing affection for the man beside her. If people took the time to get to know him, she bet they'd see there was a lot of good beneath Bradford's tough exterior.

Aly and Daphne were making their way across the room. Aly looked stunning in her deep blue gown. Head held high, she drew attention. More than one man turned to watch her stroll past.

Daphne's eyes were round, and although she looked beautiful in her gown as well, she appeared ready to bolt out of the room. Aly said something to her and she stood taller, but still afraid.

"I'm so glad you bought that dress. You look awesome," Aly said as she joined Joanna and Bradford. She hugged Joanna.

When Joanna stepped back, she said, "You do too. We'll have to go shopping together again. That was fun. I had no idea you knew so much about fashion."

Aly laughed. "Daphne, this is one of my closest friends, Joanna. She meant to say I always dress impeccably, so she was not shocked at all by my good taste in gowns."

Joanna laughed. "Yes, that's exactly what I meant." Daphne held out her hand for Joanna to shake. Giving in to an impulse, Joanna said, "I'm a big hugger. May I?"

Daphne nodded and Joanna kept her hug brief. She felt stiff at first, then relaxed. Some people had very clear physical boundaries they did not like crossed, but Joanna had discovered over the years that the more technology distanced people, the more they were hungry for human connection. *Never underestimate the healing power of a warm hug.*

Aly nodded toward Bradford in greeting. There was a

distinct chill between the two of them that saddened Joanna. When it came to diagnosing ailments, Aly was definitely the pro. When it came to things of the heart, though, Joanna liked to think she had a slight advantage.

Aly was a great friend, a wonderful doctor, and normally kind to everyone—which was why Claire had apparently entrusted her with Daphne. It was difficult to watch her with Bradford.

"Daphne, this is Bradford."

Daphne didn't offer her hand in greeting.

Nor did Bradford.

She looked afraid of him.

He looked annoyed.

More tequila anyone? "Bradford and I just did a tequila shot to ease our way into the event. Aly? Daphne? Want to join us?"

Daphne shook her head. "I d-don't. I'm not a drinker."

"Tequila," Aly cringed then turned to the bartender and asked for white wine and ginger ale. "I guess I know who I'll be driving home later."

"She thinks I can't hold my liquor." Joanna gave Bradford an elbow to the ribs. "In a drink off I would have mopped the floor with you."

"In your dreams," Bradford said in a harsh tone.

Joanna tipped her head so she could look up at him. He wasn't upset with her, so what was with the tone? He was a tough read. Was anger all he knew? "Oh, really?" She turned to the bartender. "Another round, please."

Aly intervened, "Joanna, are you sure you—?"

"I grew up sipping my grandmother's moonshine out of a teacup." Joanna picked up a shot glass, then handed one to Bradford and winked. "That's a little family secret she took to the grave, so if you ever meet my parents don't say anything."

He raised his glass as if in agreement. They both bit into their salted limes, took a sip, bit into the lime again then finished the shot. It felt like a dance of sorts that ended with her smiling up at him and him frowning down at her.

"Bradford," a male voice called from across the room. Clay Landon was walking toward them with his wife, Lexi.

"Shit," Bradford said without even turning his head in the direction of the voice.

Joanna looked back and forth between the man people said was rich enough to buy and sell the Barringtons and a seemingly irritated Bradford. "Everything okay?" Joanna asked in a low voice she hoped only he could hear.

"Yeah." Bradford flexed his shoulders then turned to face the approaching couple—smile-free, but that was expected from him.

Clay gave Bradford a back-slapping hug. "I had to pull a few strings to arrange for us to sit together. Ian's under the impression that you don't like me. I told him you don't like anyone so I don't take it personally."

At Clay's side, Lexi was beautiful, confident, and amused. "Bradford, just go with it. He hasn't come back to earth since Sophie complimented him on his success as Connor's fairy godfather."

"I can see how that might go to a man's head," Bradford

said dryly.

Joanna was fascinated by the exchange. Money apparently didn't impress Bradford nor did Clay. Clay, on the other hand, seemed to genuinely like Bradford. His endorsement was another tally in the column of why Aly's take on Bradford was inaccurate.

Clay wrapped his arm around his wife's waist. "It's all your fault, Lexi. If you didn't make me so happy, I wouldn't want to help others find their own happily ever after."

"Now that is something I don't mind taking the blame for." Lexi laid a hand on the side of his face. "You keep doing you, Clay. It's kind of sexy that you want to help people find love."

"Kind of?" Clay wiggled his eyebrows. "Like tell the nanny we won't be home tonight sexy?"

She whispered something in his ear that brought a flush to his face. In the awkward silence that followed everyone temporarily looked away.

"Clay and Lexi," Bradford said, "I'm sure you remember Joanna and Aly. And this is their—friend, Daphne."

Joanna put both hands over her heart and said, "I have heard wonderful things about you from Angelina and Connor. You have every right to celebrate that win."

Clay's chest puffed. "Thank you. See, Lexi, I was wonderful."

Lexi laughed. "You're not helping, Joanna. Compliments go straight to his head."

Clay leaned down slightly in Joanna's direction. "Lexi thinks it was a fluke—that they would have gotten together regardless. She doesn't understand the magic in what I did."

"Magic. Who couldn't use some of that?" Clay was an easy man to like. He didn't care at all about trying to impress any of them. He was who he was—no apologies.

He gave Joanna a long look. "Do you have your heart set on someone who requires a little nudge?"

Joanna flushed. The tequila shots were setting in, but not enough for her to claim Dylan publicly. "N-no."

Lexi hugged Clay. "I see what you're doing, Clay; don't think I don't. You want to find another couple you can bring together. Don't give him a name, Joanna, unless you're ready for the pumpkin coach and ball. Clay can be a little over-the-top at times." She hugged him. "It's one of the many things I love about him."

Clay waved a hand in the air. "What is a fairy godfather without a charge? Just a sad man with a magical wand."

"Poor baby," Lexi said. "We'll find you someone to help."

Joanna looked across to Aly for guidance, but she didn't offer any. *No. I can't say anything. It's one thing to dream and joke about marrying Dylan, it's another to set a plan into motion. One is harmless, the other could make things awkward for Dylan as well as Angelina, and I don't want that.*

Her eyes locked with Bradford's. Behind his seemingly practiced stare, she sensed a profound sadness that made her wish she knew him well enough to hug him and tell him everything would be okay. He could use a little of Clay's magic. She almost said that, but at the last minute she decided to keep that thought to herself as well.

The noise level in the ballroom had risen as the room filled, but when it suddenly lowered people turned to see who had arrived. Phones raised to photograph the Sutton brothers as they entered—tall, muscular, and insanely good-looking. Their huge social media following was no big mystery . . . a woman would have to be dead not to be moved a little by those two.

Angelina was holding Connor's hand. He bent to ask her something then smiled, looking so much in love with her Joanna gasped. "I want that someday," she whispered to herself.

"A Sutton?" Bradford asked in a low tone.

Joanna's gaze went to Dylan. He was certainly handsome and polished. Universally attractive. Her heart didn't race the way she'd expected it to, though. Would she feel something for him again if they spent time together? "Maybe."

Bradford walked away.

Clay looked at Lexi. "I told you tonight was worth flying in for."

She shook her head. "Clay Landon, whatever you're thinking—no."

He raised her hand to his lips and kissed the back of it. "Aly. Joanna. Daphne. We look forward to sharing a table with you, but there's something Lexi and I must do first."

"Oh, Lord," Lexi said. "See you in a few, ladies."

Joanna and the others said they looked forward to it then watched Clay and Lexi make their way across the room in the direction Bradford had gone.

Claire arrived with Ian, and Daphne scurried away to

greet her.

"I'm not going to say it," Aly said.

"Good," Joanna said lightly, "because I probably don't want to hear it."

Aly laughed. "Tequila gives you some sass."

Joanna smiled. "I suppose it does."

After a short pause, Aly said, "Drinking with Bradford; how did that happen?"

"First, we weren't 'drinking' together, we had two shots to unwind. Second, it really bothers me that you've decided you don't like him but you've never taken the time to get to know him. You're better than that, Aly."

"Whoa, let's unpack some of that. You and I tell each other everything, so asking how you and Bradford ended up downing tequila shots is not crossing any boundaries. And I never said I don't like him. I said you need to be careful with him. I've been asking around about him and no one will tell me what he does. It's concerning."

"To you. Not to me. He's been nothing but nice to me, so I don't really care what he does for a living. If it was illegal, I don't think he'd be here. Did you see how Clay Landon just fawned over him? That's enough of a reference for me. If I even required a reference before liking a person—which I don't—and nor should you."

"I hate it when you're right." Aly sighed. "I am judging him based on very little evidence, but I get this vibe from him . . ."

"What kind of vibe?"

"I shouldn't say it."

"Well you might as well now that you've brought it up."

"Like I wouldn't be surprised if I heard he'd killed someone."

"Oh, my God." Joanna scoffed. "You've watched too many crime shows. Even in those though, it's never the obvious choice who did it, so it wouldn't be him anyway."

Aly clasped her small purse in front of her. "Laugh it off, but there's something about him . . ."

"You could say that about every person in this room. Ease up." Joanna nudged her friend with her hip. "When it comes to reading people, I'm the one with the good instincts. Remember that neurosurgeon you tried to date. I told you he liked himself more than he could ever like you."

"You did call that one correctly."

"And the astrophysicist with the foot fetish. Come on, you thought he liked you barefoot just because he preferred shorter women. No way. I saw the way he checked out my tootsies when I wore sandals."

Aly laughed. "You win. You are definitely a better reader of men. Maybe I'm wrong about Bradford. I hope I am."

"You are." Joanna searched the room until she spotted Bradford. Their eyes met and held. "He's not dangerous, Aly, just sad. I see that expression in the eyes of throw-away horses all the time. He's shut down. Someone hurt him, maybe threw him away too. He looks angry because he's probably learned it's safer to keep people at a distance, but if you look past that you see something else. He's here to support the Barringtons and they adore him. That says all I need to know about who he is on the inside."

"You almost sound interested in him. Have you given up on Dylan?"

"Bradford and I are just friends." Reluctantly, she dragged her gaze away from Bradford and sought out Dylan in the crowd. He was surrounded by a circle of adoring women. It was fun for Joanna to fantasize about being with him, having him choose her above all those beautiful women, but it was becoming more difficult to imagine being with him. "Do you think he's as nice as Connor or has his celebrity status gone to his head?"

One of the women with him said something that made Dylan laugh. He appeared to love all the attention he was receiving. Aly sighed. "I'm sure even a humble person has a difficult time remaining that way when all they hear is how wonderful they are. Unending praise is not good for anyone."

"So I definitely shouldn't flatter him."

Without looking away from Dylan, Aly said, "Not unless you want to become part of that herd."

"I don't." Joanna looked around the room. It was quickly filling with the rich and famous. When Sophie Barrington threw a charity ball anyone who was anyone showed up.

With Connor on her arm, Angelina made mingling look effortless. Neither had come from money nor even gone looking for it, but Connor's sister, Viviana, had married into the Barrington family and that meant events like this were now part of their lives. *Which doesn't mean it needs to be part of mine. I'm already happy with my life.* "Although it would have been fun to have a fairy godfather."

Chapter Three

"**B**RADFORD," Clay called out as he approached with his wife.

I should have left when I had the chance. Bradford straightened to his full height. He didn't say anything because silence often spoke louder than words.

Most men found Bradford intimidating, sadly Clay wasn't one of them. "Could I have a moment of your time?"

"No."

Clay smiled at Lexi. "He's funny, isn't he?"

Lexi gave Bradford a long look, then gripped her husband's arm. "This is a bad idea."

After giving her hand a reassuring pat, Clay said, "Every new idea is doubted at first but then they work out and are considered genius."

Bradford shook his head. "I could list countless times ideas took a much darker path."

Clay clapped a hand on Bradford's arm. "Then you'll just have to trust me."

Leaning in, Bradford growled, "Don't fucking touch me." He straightened and frowned.

Lexi looked from him to her husband and back. "Do you want me to call Clay off?"

"You do realize I can hear you?" Clay asked with amused sarcasm.

"No, I can handle this." Bradford looked Clay in the eye. "What do you want, Clay?"

Clay waved a hand in the air. "You're right. This is a conversation we should have alone." He smiled down at his wife. "Lexi, do you mind giving us a few minutes?"

She bit her bottom lip. "Clay—"

"It'll be fine," Clay assured her.

"Are you sure?"

"I am. Now let me work my magic."

She nodded then went up onto her tiptoes to give him a kiss. When she stepped back she looked at Bradford and said, "Clay only gets involved when he cares."

Bradford waited until she walked beyond hearing distance before he said, "No, Clay."

"You don't even know what I'm about to say."

"I don't have to. Whatever it is, I'm not interested."

"But you are. You can lie to everyone else, possibly even yourself, but a fairy godfather knows all."

"I can't kill you, but I want to."

Clay threw back his head and laughed. "I get that a lot."

Bradford rubbed a hand over his temple. "There are a hundred other people in this room. Some of them may even want to speak to you. You should seek them out."

"So, you're just going to sit back and watch Joanna hook up with Dylan?"

Bradford's eyes narrowed but he didn't respond. His hands clenched at his sides.

Clay continued, "I got the impression you were interested in her, but I've been wrong before. Wait, no, I haven't. My track record is solid. You're totally into her. What's the problem?"

"This conversation is over."

"Do you have someone already? Someone you haven't told us about? A marriage you meant to dissolve but haven't?"

I'm not fucking doing this. Bradford could have walked away then, but that would have handed a win to Clay. Instead he folded his arms across his chest and stared forward, dismissing him.

It should have worked. Clay was relentless though. "If it's not that, what is it? She's sweet, smart, liked by everyone. Sure, her taste in men seems a little shallow, but the Suttons are beefy eye candy. You can't fault her for not noticing you when they're around. Don't take this the wrong way, but you—"

"Get the fuck away from me."

"You have to admit you're a little rough around the edges. Women are understanding though. Let her see your softer side. You do have one, don't you?"

Bradford growled deep in his throat.

Clay nodded. "We can work on that later. For now, follow my lead. I already have a few ideas."

With his self-control stretched to near the breaking point, Bradford took a deep breath and reminded himself that he had survived much worse. There was the time in South America when he'd been arrested by police who were on a drug cartel's payroll. He'd maintained his silence even through their brutal methods to get him to say who he was working with. He'd been a bloody mess by the time Ian had rescued him, but he'd given up nothing beyond his first name. *Clay is an annoyance, a fly buzzing around my head.*

Difficult to ignore, but of no importance.

"Bradford!" an older woman exclaimed as she approached. Sophie Barrington was dressed tastefully as always, understated but classic. She wore wealth well. When she stopped in front of him she took both of his hands in hers, a move that always made him feel cornered. Still, he didn't pull away from her. He had yet to see her say a bad word about anyone. Violence was a necessary response against evil, but it had no place next to such a gentle soul. "Thank you for coming."

He ducked his head in acknowledgement of her appreciation.

She released his hands and turned to Clay. "Are you starting trouble with Bradford?"

Clay bent to kiss Sophie on the cheek. "Me? At one of your events? Never."

She smiled but wagged a finger at him. "Clay Landon look me in the eye and tell me you're not up to something."

After shrugging one shoulder, Clay said, "I'm always up to something—but so are you and I love you more for it."

Sophie arched an eyebrow then returned her attention to Bradford. "Have you seen Joanna tonight? Doesn't she look darling in that gown?"

"I hadn't noticed," Bradford said.

Clay scoffed. "Sure, we'll go with that."

"She's single," Sophie added with a smile.

Let me clarify this for those who are confused. "I'm not in the market for a relationship."

Sophie sighed. "I heard she's sweet on Dylan, but I don't see them as a good match. She's too nice for him. She needs someone who would treasure her, protect her. Someone who wouldn't see her soft heart as a weakness."

With his chest puffing with pride, Clay said, "Great minds think alike, Sophie. I was just offering to help Bradford win her heart."

Bradford swore beneath his breath.

Sophie made a tsk sound. "Well, that explains Bradford's pained expression. Clay, this is a situation that requires more subtlety than that. Let me handle this."

"There is no situation," Bradford said.

"Sophie," Clay said with a smooth smile, "are you doubting my abilities? My success rate is one hundred percent."

"Excuse me. I have to—" Bradford didn't finish the sentence because what he had to do was extricate himself from the conversation. He turned on his heel and took a step away.

"Bradford," Sophie said quickly.

He paused and looked over his shoulder. "Yes?"

"Stay and enjoy the event. Please. It means a lot to me that you're here."

He was tempted to tell her he didn't care how she felt

about anything, but Sophie had never been anything but warm and welcoming to him. He nodded once, then turned again and strode away.

Behind him, Clay called out, "See you at the table, Bradford."

Yeah, that wasn't going to happen. Out of respect for Sophie, Bradford would stay, but that didn't mean he needed to obediently take his seat and endure more of Clay Landon's ramblings.

Idiot.

He scanned the room for Joanna. She was in the process of taking her seat at their table. Aly was on her left. Daphne left of her. Clay and Lexi were next to them as well as Connor and Angelina. There were two open seats at the table—one for Bradford and one for Dylan.

Which seat had Sophie assigned directly next to Joanna? Bradford hadn't checked and he told himself it didn't matter since he had no intention of joining them anyway.

It wasn't difficult to spot Dylan. Even as he walked across the room, several women flanked him. When he reached the table, he bent to say something to Joanna then introduced her to the hovering crowd. A moment later the women dispersed and Dylan took the seat beside Joanna.

She seemed distracted as he spoke to her, looking around the room rather than at him. Bradford stayed in the shadows. He wasn't what she was seeking, and even if he was, he certainly wasn't what she needed.

He flexed his hands at his side. It wasn't easy to watch Dylan lean closer to speak to Joanna, but he refused to validate that feeling. Life was full of difficult decisions and each one a person made came with consequences. There was a time, a long, long time ago, when he might have yearned for the "normal" life Joanna represented. The man he'd become had no such dreams.

There's too much blood on my hands.

Too many reasons Joanna would be a lot better off with a man like Dylan.

Even though Bradford gave the Suttons shit, they were actually some of the nicest people he'd ever come across. Sean Sutton, a construction company owner from Upstate New York had raised his three children on his own after his wife died. His daughter, Viviana, was the tough little cookie who'd married Grant Barrington. Connor and Dylan were comically simple, but loyal to their core. They were the first to laugh at themselves when they stumbled and easy to like. Clay and Sophie were wrong . . . Joanna didn't need protecting, she needed someone who was as nice as she was. Grudgingly, Bradford conceded to himself that Dylan wouldn't be a bad match for her.

Joanna's gaze locked with Bradford's. She waved for him to join them. He didn't budge.

She frowned.

Trust me, sweetheart, I'm doing you a favor.

"THANKS FOR HELPING me out, Joanna. I didn't think I'd be able to shake them. One of them slipped me a hotel key with her name and number on it. I like sex but I can only have so much on one trip." Dylan sighed. "I'm exhausted."

Without looking away from Bradford, Joanna said, "Glad I could help." Why was he standing with the event's security detail rather than sitting at the table? *Was it something I said?*

Or something I did?

At almost every Barrington gathering she'd seen him at, Bradford stood apart, looking as if he didn't feel he belonged there. Her heart went out to him. It wasn't that no one attempted to draw him in. Sophie and Dale always made a point of personally welcoming Bradford. He was the best friend of their son Ian. He belonged—even if he didn't believe it.

Dylan continued, "There are times when I welcome the attention, but then at events like this it would be easier to come with someone so I could relax and enjoy myself."

"Sure. Anytime," Joanna said absently.

"I may take you up on that."

A thought occurred to Joanna. "Dylan, go see if you can get Bradford to join us."

Dylan turned in his seat to look in the direction she was. "Bradford does what Bradford wants. It's best not to push him."

Connor chimed in from across the table. "Dylan's afraid of him."

"I am not," Dylan said. "There's a difference between fearing someone and having a healthy respect for them. I like him, but no one wants to be on his bad side."

Aly asked, "Why? What happens if you are?"

Connor and Dylan exchanged a look then a laugh. With

a wink, Connor said, "Let's just say we could tell you but then we'd have to kill you."

Aly's eyes widened.

Angelina playfully smacked Connor's arm. "Stop. Bradford is wonderful. He even checks in on Mrs. Tellier because she lives alone and has been having health issues. That's sweet."

Dylan chuckled. "Sweet? Bradford? Sure."

Bradford still checked in on Mrs. Tellier. It had been Bradford who had made sure Mrs. Tellier was okay after Angelina had been fired for coming to her defense against the horrible headmaster of the school where they'd both worked. It had also been Bradford who had encouraged Connor to hire Mrs. Tellier. To hear that he was still checking on her warmed Joanna's heart. Aly was so wrong about him. "Connor," Joanna said, "do you think you could encourage him to join us?"

With an easy smile, Connor rose to his feet. "Absolutely. I'll be right back, Angelina." He gave her a quick parting kiss before turning to his brother. "You coming, Dylan?"

"Nah, you've got this." Once Connor was out of earshot, Dylan added, "Bradford really likes Connor. Me? Not so much."

"I'm sure that's not true," Joanna said.

"It's true," Clay interjected.

Lexi laughed. "Clay, that's not nice to say."

"The truth often isn't." Clay shrugged. "Joanna, what do you think of Bradford?"

Before answering, Joanna exchanged a look with Aly. "I

think he's worth taking the time to get to know."

Aly's eyebrows rose and fell, but she nodded in concession. "Tonight's an opportunity for that to happen, so let's hope Connor is successful."

Dylan laid an arm across the back of Joanna's chair. "That's probably what it is—Connor has just had more time with him. I'm going to make more of an effort."

Clay laughed. "You can try, but if you're looking to be his friend you're going about it entirely the wrong way."

Dylan looked over his shoulder in the direction of his departing brother. "You're right, I should have gone with him. Connor has always been better than I am at liking people until they cave and like him back. I've always admired that about him."

Joanna's attention shifted back to Dylan and she realized he was sitting much closer than he had been. She took a moment to appreciate the perfection of his features and how the broad expanse of his chest filled her field of vision. She expected her heart to race, but it didn't. Disappointing. He truly was beautiful and worthy of a fantasy or two, but the zing she'd hoped to feel hadn't come.

That didn't mean she couldn't sympathize with him. Connor had shared his struggle to fit in with the Barrington family and how he still craved the simple life he'd had before his sister had married into money. Dylan likely felt the same. His jokes might well be based in truth. One of the women from earlier walked by the table and attempted to gain his attention. He shifted even closer to Joanna. If he kept it up, he'd soon be in her lap. "Everyone thinks they want to be a celebrity, but it's not easy, is it?"

Dylan let out an audible breath. "I'm not complaining." He nodded toward Clay. "I'm grateful for everything. Clay pretty much handed me a movie career."

Clay leaned forward. "I made an introduction. You did the rest. You have a lot to be proud of."

Dylan nodded. "Thanks. I just don't want to fuck it up."

Joanna put a hand on his forearm. "You won't. I've seen *Danger Doubled*. You're a natural."

His smile was as likeable as Connor's. Honest. Simple. "Things were a lot easier when no one knew my name. I used to be jealous that Connor got laid more often than I did. Everything came so easy to him. I don't even think half those women want to fuck *me*—they just want to say they did."

Aly sputtered, "Disgusting."

Dylan looked around Joanna. "Hey, no one was talking to you, peanut gallery."

"Thank God," Aly answered, "because I have zero tolerance for bullshit."

"Bullshit? Why don't you go read the book you probably have on your phone."

"What are you mocking? That I *read*?" Aly sat forward, going nose to nose with Dylan right in front of Joanna.

"If the shoe fits."

"That doesn't even make sense. And you can't mock something that's good."

"Oh, sorry, I didn't memorize the rules of what could and couldn't be mocked."

"I should let you two—" Joanna would have moved out from between the two, but they'd blocked her in.

"Are you really that dumb?" Aly asked.

Joanna cringed.

"Are you really that judgmental?"

Aly gasped. "I'm not judgmental."

Dylan moved his head back and forth in front of hers. "Didn't like that, did you? I just judged you for judging me. See how I turned that right around?"

"Whatever," Aly sat back. "I shouldn't have said anything."

"No," Dylan said, still talking around Joanna. "Say whatever you want, but know that this is why I asked Joanna and not you to be my fake date tonight."

"What?" Joanna sat up straighter. "When did you ask me that?"

"When I came over and introduced you to those women."

"You asked me if this was where we were sitting."

"Exactly, *we*. The rest was implied. And you agreed."

"I—I—"

"Too late now," Dylan said. "They all think we're a couple. Unless you want to break up with me in public."

Joanna opened her mouth, then closed it when she wasn't sure how to respond to that.

Angelina piped in, "Fake dating. That's kind of cute. Who knows, maybe we could fake double date one day." She winked at Joanna.

Joanna looked at Dylan. There was nothing not to like

about him. Half the women in the room would have given a kidney to be sitting where Joanna was. She'd spent a good deal of time fantasizing about what it would be like to be with him—in any capacity. *So, what's wrong with me? Why am I not jumping at this opportunity?*

He gave her the charming smile she'd seen him use on the big screen. No flutter. Nothing. Still, there wasn't a reason she couldn't help him. "You seriously don't want to hook up with any of those women?" she asked.

Dylan relaxed. "I seriously don't. I want to enjoy hanging out with everyone tonight. With them I have to be Dylan Sutton, the movie star. I have to watch everything I say. I just want to be me for a couple of hours."

"Okay." Joanna nodded. "Just this once and don't announce anything we'll have to deny later. I'm fine with us looking like we're together, but if Sophie or anyone asks we're not."

"Good enough for me. Thanks Joanna."

"Well, this should be interesting," Clay said.

"What?" Joanna asked.

"Connor is walking over with Bradford."

Chapter Four

I SHOULD HAVE said no.

There is no sane reason why I belong at that table.

So why the hell didn't I just lie and say I was working the event?

Bradford wasn't a kind man, not even to himself. It was time to wake the fuck up from whatever spell Joanna had cast over him. If sitting there while she hung all over Dylan was what it took, then so be it. He came to a stop right behind Dylan.

Arm still around the back of Joanna's chair, Dylan smiled up at him. "You snooze, you lose, Bradford. I stole your seat."

Don't react. Over the years Bradford had become very good at keeping his feelings about anything to himself. "It's all yours."

Joanna searched his face then said, "I'm glad you decided to join us."

Bradford sat in the seat that still had a place card for Dylan. He picked the card up, gathered every last feeling he had about the situation, stuffed it deep in his gut and closed the door to it all while crumpling the card in his fist.

"Me too," Dylan said. "I'm around for a couple of weeks before I have to return to finish shooting. We should hang out."

The silence he offered Dylan was better than the first few responses that had come to Bradford. He had to remind himself that he didn't hate Dylan.

Connor said, "I have some time before my next movie starts, we should definitely plan something together."

Yeah, no.

Angelina chimed in, "Aly? Joanna? What do you say? Could you take some time off—get a house on a lake or something?"

"I could free up some time," Aly said.

"Sounds fun. I'm not sure how much time I could take off. I'll have to get someone to watch my farm, but I'm sure I can make something happen," Joanna added. She looked across to Daphne who had yet to say a word at the table. "Daphne, you should join us."

"Oh, I don't know," Daphne said, keeping her eyes glued to the table. "I appreciate you letting me sit with you, but I know that doesn't make us friends."

"Say yes," Joanna said with a warm smile. "I promise you won't regret it."

Daphne nodded. "Okay. If you're serious. I'd love to join you."

"Great, that's settled then." Joanna turned and addressed Bradford. "You too. Everyone needs a vacation now and then."

He opened his mouth to say he couldn't, but Clay cut him off. "I have an idea. We should head back with Dylan to Iceland and watch him on set. I say we all head over, watch him in action, and stay long enough to celebrate the completion of his first solo movie. What do you say, Dylan?"

"I'd love that," Dylan said. "It won't take very long. I'm redoing some scenes then it's a wrap."

Clay clapped his hands. "Perfect. Two weeks. That gives everyone time to clear their schedules. Leave the travel details and lodging to me." He nudged Lexi. "By me, I mean Lexi, she's better at it than I am. What do you say, Lexi?"

His wife smiled up at him. "I think you're playing with fire, my darling husband, but I'm in. I've never been to Iceland. This is exciting."

"My friend Jón owns an island in Ísafjarðardjúp Bay in the Westfjords. It used to be open to tours, but he's made it into a private residence. He's hardly ever there. It's mostly farmland run by the caretaker. Cows. Goats. Horses too, if I remember correctly. It'd be the perfect location to celebrate the wrap-up of Dylan's movie."

"Icelandic horses?" Joanna's face lit up. "I wonder if we could do trail rides."

"I'm sure we can," Clay said then nuzzled Lexi's cheek. "You can set that up, right?"

Lexi laughed. "What would you do without me?"

Clay shuddered. "I don't even want to imagine it. You're stuck with me."

She kissed him. "Happily." She looked around. "Okay, so for planning purposes, we're all in?"

One by one everyone except Bradford said they were. All eyes turned to him.

Connor said, "Bradford, you have to come. If you think the catfish are big here, you should see what you can catch out there."

Dylan cleared his throat. "You've probably been on a hundred sets, but it would mean a lot to me if you came out to see me in action. I've been doing all my own stunts and half the time I can't believe I haven't killed myself doing them, but it's so cool to see the difference between what I actually do and how it appears in the movie."

Bradford groaned. Why did Dylan need to be so damned likable? "I have obligations—"

"We all do," Connor said, "but you can't not come, Bradford. Any day now Angelina is going to start popping out babies and we won't be able to get together like this."

"Really?" Angelina asked with amusement. "Just popping them out?"

Connor shrugged. "You know what I mean. Travel is easier before children."

"What is Whitney?"

Connor blushed at Angelina's mention of her son. "I don't think of him like a kid? You know he's always welcome."

Angelina's eyebrow arched then she laughed. "I love giving you shit. Whitney has soccer camp anyway. Given the choice between hanging out with old people or working on his kicks, you know what he'd pick."

Joanna peered around Dylan. "Come on, Bradford. We

can try Brennivín. I hear it tastes like vodka." She wiggled her eyebrows. "And you can show off your equestrian skills."

"Do you know how to ride?" Connor asked.

Did riding with the Kazakh nomads in the Altai Mountains in Mongolia count? There, horses were essential for survival in a way of life that was quickly becoming a thing of the past. A few years back he'd spent a month herding yaks, goats, and sheep after word had gotten out that the government was trying to eliminate their migration route. A private company was interested in buying the land the nomads used to graze their herds and were using violent poachers to intimidate them. Bradford corrected the situation. *So, yeah, I can ride.* "Enough to stay on a horse."

"I knew it," Joanna said. "I've never been to Iceland so all of this sounds amazing. Bradford, you have to come."

Clay jumped in. "That's settled then. Lexi, plan for nine of us. Fishing. Riding. Thermal baths. I love Iceland."

"Eight," Bradford said in a tone that discouraged debate.

No one said anything for a moment, then Clay said, "Eight it is."

"Seven," Daphne said. "Really, I appreciate the offer, but travel brings out my anxiety."

Dylan joked, "And that's why this group is good for me—you all trim my ego right down. We don't have to make our time together about me. The lake house idea also sounded cool."

"No," Clay said while looking Bradford right in the eye. "We all know how seriously you take your new career. You found something you enjoy and you went for it. It's sad how many people don't have the balls to go after what they want."

"Don't go there," Bradford said between clenched teeth.

"Boys," Lexi said, "do I have to go get Sophie?"

Clay smiled and sat back. "No need. My point has been made."

Joanna turned to Dylan. "What did I miss?"

"I have no idea." Dylan raised both hands in confusion.

Bradford leaned forward. He'd sworn he wouldn't allow himself to lose control, but his temper was flaring. His mood wasn't helped by how comfortable Joanna was looking with Dylan. More of that in Iceland? No thanks. Since he couldn't say that, Bradford said, "Clay, have you considered that my schedule might not be as open as yours?"

Without missing a beat, Clay asked, "Have you considered you might be a coward?"

Bradford pushed back his chair and stood.

Joanna rose to her feet. "Bradford."

It was too late, Bradford had already turned and begun to walk away. He didn't pause at the feel of her hand on his arm. "Go back to the table, Joanna."

"Not without you. Clay was pushing your buttons. We all saw it. He owes you an apology."

Bradford paused and looked down at the woman who had been trotting to keep up with him. "He owes me nothing; just like I owe him nothing. Don't waste your time on a situation that really doesn't matter. You have what you want—Dylan is all over you tonight. You might want to stay focused on closing that deal before you find your seat taken as well."

"First, this does matter. You're obviously upset."

In a low tone, Bradford growled, "To be upset I'd have to give a shit about anyone here. I don't."

Joanna put her hands on her hips, a move that pushed her breasts higher than her bodice in a highly distracting way. He didn't want to be turned on by her, but it seemed all she had to do was breathe next to him for his cock to take notice. "I don't believe you."

He glared at her. She had Dylan. Was she the kind of woman who needed every man around her to validate that she was beautiful?

She continued, "I know you care about Ian."

He let out a slow breath, holding her gaze without speaking.

"And Connor. Even Dylan. I know you like them."

He couldn't hold back anymore. "What the fuck do you want from me, Joanna?"

Her expression softened. "I want you to admit you care and then I want to get you that apology."

"Don't get involved. Although I appreciate you coming to my defense, I can fight my own battles. Clay's an idiot. I shouldn't have let him get under my skin. That's on me."

Joanna's hands dropped to her sides. "The funny thing is I think he really wants you to go."

"I'm sure he does."

"Connor and Dylan adore you. Angelina thinks you're wonderful. She was saying how much it means to her that you still check in on Mrs. Tellier. They all want you there."

Not happening.

"I do too."

Her softly spoken declaration knocked the breath clear out of him. He scrambled to raise his defenses. It would be so easy, too easy to pull her close and kiss those sweet lips of hers. "You need to stay away from me, Joanna," he said in a guttural tone.

She took a step back. "I'm just trying to be your friend."

"I've got all the friends I need," Bradford said, turning and walking away, but not before he'd glimpsed hurt and confusion fill her expression. He felt like a total ass. It wasn't her fault he found it difficult to think straight around her. She deserved better than how he'd treated her.

Ian met him just outside the door of the ballroom. "You're not leaving already, are you?"

Bradford shook his hand. "Tell your mother something came up that required my attention."

"You okay? I saw Clay chasing after you like a moth to a flame, but you usually brush him off easily enough. I knew it was a mistake to seat you at the same table."

Flexing his shoulders, Bradford admitted, "Clay wasn't the problem in there, I was. My head is all fucked up tonight."

"Anything you need to talk about?"

"I'll be fine by tomorrow."

"I heard things got complicated in Libya."

"No more than usual; the son of the US ambassador lingered behind too long. He was trapped on the wrong side of the siege lines, but luckily for him the insurgent militia didn't know who he was. He's back with his parents now, a little humbler but unscathed." Bradford frowned. "Why do you know about it at all?"

"A perk of being on the right side of the government. I keep tabs on you and those who would like to see you gone. In some circles you're considered a national treasure."

"I'm sure."

"In others—well, I won't bore you with how many times I talk people out of attempting to erase you. Remember when we thought no one knew what we did? They knew. Be careful, Bradford. You've taken on some dangerous targets since I stepped away."

"I'm doing what we've always done."

"Yes, but with less caution. Don't get yourself killed or I'll feel guilty about leaving you for the quieter life."

Bradford rolled his eyes. "Good to see you, Ian." Just then his phone beeped with a message from Clay.

I went too far. I'm sorry.

In response, he typed: **Is this really Clay?**

It's me, but I do have Joanna standing over me telling me what to write.

Bradford choked on a laugh, then gave into it.

Ian stepped closer. "What's so funny?"

Bradford shook his head and pocketed his phone. "The irony of life." It was all he'd say on the matter. "I'll be in touch."

"I'll be watching. If you need me I'm always just one encrypted, highly classified text message away."

"Good to know," Bradford said as he turned away. "Same. You know how to find me if you need me."

On the walk through the lobby, Bradford imagined Joanna cornering Clay and demanding he send an apology. She couldn't sit back and say nothing when she saw an injustice. *Looks like we have something in common after all.*

Joanna was the first woman in—forever—that Bradford felt a connection with. He couldn't find a damn thing he didn't like about her.

So, what do I do?

I push her away.

"You snooze, you lose." Dylan's early taunt came back to haunt Bradford.

Clay's question quickly followed. "Have you considered you might be a coward?"

Rather than taking his car, Bradford decided to walk and return for his vehicle later. As he walked, his past nipped at his heels.

One street led to another as memories overtook him. Too vividly he remembered himself at seven holding his older sister Ella's hand in the hospital when they were told that neither of their parents had survived. "Let this be a lesson to you, son," a police officer had told him. "Bad things happen when you get mixed up with the wrong people."

Bradford had been too young to understand, but the words had cut. He knew his parents had been shot by someone they sold drugs for, but not much compassion was shown for him or his sister as they dealt with the loss. Because of their ages and the fact that they were considered affiliated with local gangs, they were separated and sent to homes outside the city.

Ella had run away from her foster family and back to the only life she knew. Bradford lost touch with her until he was old enough to also return to his old neighborhood. When he found his sister he barely recognized her. The same gang she'd turned to for protection had gotten her addicted to drugs then pimped her out.

In his teens Bradford had been too young to take them on. He'd tried and been beaten within an inch of his life and left for dead. Some of the scars on his face were from that beating, some were more recent. Although they prevented him from ever being called handsome, he didn't mind them. Each scar was its own badge of honor. When he recovered from that first beating, he'd sworn he'd pull Ella out of that life. The scar from a bullet that narrowly missed his heart was from his second attempt to save her. Ella died of a drug overdose while he was still in the hospital recovering.

If there was a hero in his life back then it had been his foster father, Alan. Neither he nor his wife were what one would call nurturing. They believed tough love made strong adults. Although Bradford wouldn't say they were what he needed back then, he respected them for never giving up on him. Bradford was a ball of fury after Ella died. Still, Alan and his wife kept him. He thought it was for the paycheck, but looking back there must have been easier kids to foster.

When Bradford aged out of the foster program, Alan encouraged him to enlist in the Army. "Want to fight? Fight for your country. Want to die? Die saving someone."

It wasn't exactly an inspirational speech, but it had stuck

with Bradford. He didn't see much value to his own life, but he'd spent the last decade fighting for the vulnerable. He'd taken some tangents off that noble path to settle some scores. Every last gang member who had been a part of his parents' or his sister's deaths had found quick and brutal justice at Bradford's hands.

One might argue that the world was a better place without them, but Bradford felt that whatever good might have been in him had died along with those he'd terminated. The only thing that kept him from putting a gun to his own head each morning was the face of each innocent he'd saved. Each woman he freed from an abusive situation, and sadly the sex trade was still very much alive and kicking even in the United States, gave him a reason to keep going. Every time he returned a child to their parents he was called a hero, but he never felt like one.

He felt tired. Ian was right; he'd spent a good amount of the last year taking bigger risks, facing down the vilest of demons. He'd seen things that would haunt him for the rest of his life—done things as well.

During one particularly ugly mission a single mother and toddler had been kidnapped by a serial killer the police had been tracking but were unable to catch. When Bradford found them, the mother was tied up and had been raped. The child was crying in the next room. Bradford killed the killer, but first let him beg for his life. It wasn't until he freed the woman and saw how he had made her afraid of him as well that he realized he was becoming as coldhearted as the criminals he erased.

Like an alcoholic pouring his liquor stash down the sink, Bradford had sworn that day to only kill when there was no other option. He'd begun working more with his contacts in law enforcement—in the US and around the globe. In some ways it was more complicated, but it also allowed him to breathe for the first time in years.

The woman he'd saved? Although he'd had no further contact with her, he'd made sure she and her son received assistance. She was now living in a small town in Maine and was taking courses at a local college. He had people check on her now and then. She'd never know of his involvement, but he'd set up support for her and her child so if they ever needed a little boost there would always be someone to step in and help out.

I'm trying to be a better person.

I have a fucking long way to go.

Joanna didn't belong with someone like him. A smile twisted his mouth as he imagined her standing over Clay and telling him what to type. Was she always that bold?

He was lost in his thoughts when three men stepped out of an alley he'd just passed. "Look what we have here. Going to a party?" one asked.

Without looking up, Bradford said, "You don't want to do this."

There was the flash of a blade then another of the men said, "Throw me your wallet. And that watch."

Bradford assessed the three young men and said, "Fair warning. You come for me and the one with the knife is the first to feel my fist." He pointed to the next man. "You'll piss yourself from the ass kicking I'll give you." And then the third. "And you're dumb enough to try to jump me while I'm dealing with them so you'll definitely get shot. I'm in a really bad mood tonight. If I were you I'd walk away."

It might have been the scars on his face that lent credibility to his claim or the gun he made sure he flashed as he spoke. He didn't care which. Or maybe a man who has nothing to lose and no chance of getting into heaven has a certain look in his eye.

The one Bradford was sure would get shot said, "Bring it on."

"He has a gun," the man with the knife said.

It was almost amusing to see how quickly the man Bradford guessed would piss himself backed down. He said, "It's not worth it, guys. Come on, let's go."

They hesitated, seemed to weigh their options, then turned to leave. Bradford sighed, took out his phone, and used an app that scanned their phones for their identification. He sent that information along with details of what had happened to his friend on the local police force. Someone needed to make sure those three didn't simply pick an easier victim.

He was in the process of putting his phone away when it beeped with a message. He expected to see a question from the detective he'd contacted, but instead it was a text from Joanna.

If you're done pouting by then—we could meet for breakfast. There's a diner next to J.D. Field Park in Doler, New Jersey. On Log Road. The park has a path that loops around the pond. I know you have all the friends you need, but I'm

talking about pancakes with blueberries the size of eyeballs. Hang on, that doesn't sound as delicious as I tried to make it sound. Anyway, they use huge blueberries.

He imagined her as he read the text. She would be smiling, those beautiful eyes of hers dancing with humor. He gave in to the smile pulling at his lips. **I don't pout.**

Good then there's no reason you can't meet me.

Not a good idea. **Except I don't eat breakfast.**

Never?

Never.

Do you walk?

I do, but I have plans for the morning.

Liar.

He choked on a laugh. He was lying, but he wasn't used to people calling him out like that. **Ask Dylan. I'm sure he'd love to go.** He groaned as he read his text. God, he sounded like a jealous teenager. He was right not to get involved with her. She was kryptonite for his brain.

I could ask him. Would you come if he says yes? I could also ask Connor and Angelina. We could go for a little hike, all skip breakfast, and have an early lunch.

Oh my God, this woman has no clue. He was preparing to type a simple, "No." when she wrote: **Please.**

What the fuck? **Why are you doing this?**

I like you.

No. That's not what this is. **And?**

And Dylan really was excited for all of us to go to Iceland to see the end of his filming. Can't you reconsider? I'll make sure Clay doesn't go after you again.

She thinks Clay is the reason that trip is on my hell-no list? **I'm not worried about Clay and I have no desire to see Iceland.**

Dylan will be so sad. He wants to spend more time with you.

Bradford typed, **"I don't give a fuck what Dylan wants"** then deleted it. He told himself not to ask, but he had to know. **Are you still at the event?**

Yes, but I'm in the foyer.

I wouldn't make Dylan wait too long.

Are you mad at me?

No.

You're not being nice.

I'm not a nice person.

Wow. That's lame. So, instead of trying to do better you're embracing being rude?

Bradford sighed. **You can stop texting me anytime you want, sweetheart.**

Pretend I just typed a gagging emoji. I don't know which one that is, but if I did I would have typed it. Men should never say sweetheart unless they mean it and you need to apologize to me. I've been nothing but nice to you.

That wasn't true. She'd also been painfully distracting, sweet enough to make him wish he were a better man, and so damn frustrating he was torn between telling her to stay the hell away from him or asking her to meet him at his place.

I already know she'd ignore the former.

What would she do with the latter?

She added: **I'm waiting.**

He had to reread her text before that one to remember what she was waiting for.

If I apologize will you stop texting me? Sure, it was a dick comment, but he needed to end the conversation before she caught on to how easily she tied him up in knots.

Wow. No, I'll stop without an apology. Sorry, I was just trying to help.

Don't fucking apologize. *Not when I'm being an ass.*

I'm going to get you a swear jar. Then every time you curse you'll have to put money in it.

Was she serious? **I'd be broke within a week.**

Not necessarily. My parents used to let me take a quarter out of our swear jar every time I did something nice for someone. They wanted me to see that mistakes happen but there's always a way back.

If only life were that simple. Maybe it's time she gets a taste of who I really am. **I was in second grade when my parents died during a drug deal that went bad. No one gave a shit what came out of my mouth back then. No one dares to tell me what I can or can't say now.**

She took a moment to answer. **I'm sorry you went through that. Life isn't fair. I know there's nothing I can say that could make whatever you've been through okay, but I do care.**

He didn't have an immediate response to that. He was a tangled mess on the inside and it was her fault. She made him feel things he hadn't in a long time and he didn't like it. **Fair enough.**

I have an extra jar at home. I'll make a sign for it.

Holy shit. **Don't bother.**

It's no bother. You might find you like it. I'll bring it to breakfast tomorrow morning.

I won't be there.

That's okay, I will be.

He held the phone up in front of him and shook it. He didn't text anything after that.

I'm not meeting you for breakfast.

I'll swear as much as I fucking want to whenever I fucking want to.

I don't want your fucking jar.

There isn't a way back—not for me.

JOANNA STOOD IN the foyer smiling down at her phone. *See you in the morning, Bradford. I'll make you that jar because it's fun and you need some of that in your life.*

Angelina walked out of the ballroom. As soon as she spotted Joanna she headed over to her. "Everything okay?"

Dropping her phone back in her small clutch, Joanna nodded. "Just getting a little air."

"I was half-afraid you might have left. Things looked like they got heated when you were talking to Clay and Lexi."

Joanna wrinkled her nose. "I'm sorry. I couldn't not say something. I thought he owed Bradford an apology."

With a pained look, Angelina said, "I should have said something as well. It's just that Clay has done so much for Connor and—"

"You don't have to explain, Ange. The whole situation was confusing. Clay told me he likes Bradford even if it doesn't appear that way. I don't understand what he was trying to do, but we both agreed he handled it badly."

A smile spread across Angelina's face. "I need another moment to soak in the fact that my best friend made Clay Landon apologize to someone."

"It helped that his wife was on my side."

"Lexi is so down-to-earth, isn't she? You've met her twin, Willa."

"Lance's wife?"

"Yes. Polar opposites. Willa is calm, soft spoken. She said Lexi was a ball of trouble before she met Clay. Love has a way of bringing out the best in people."

"It sure does. I love watching you with Connor. You make me believe in soul mates."

Angelina's cheeks went pink. "I never imagined love could be this good. I can finally be myself and not worry if that's good enough. He says it's the same for him. I was nervous coming here tonight, but so was he . . . so we're here for each other."

"I love that. I'm so happy for the two of you. I hope to one day find the same with someone."

"You were looking pretty cozy with Dylan. Do you think your fake date will lead to something real?"

Joanna adjusted her dress. "I don't think so. I like him, but not enough to take it there."

Angelina's eyebrows rose. "Last time we talked you were really into him."

"I was into the idea of him. Besides, did you see Aly and Dylan argue? Was it me or did the air sizzle?"

"It sizzled," Angelina agreed. "I'll admit I was a little worried when I saw them going at each other. She's normally so cool and collected. I did wonder if she might have feelings for him. I don't want to see either of you get hurt."

"Well now I wish I'd said no to the fake date. Should I say something to her?"

"I would. Maybe not at the table or even tonight, but soon. Before Iceland."

"Definitely." Joanna took a moment to imagine Dylan and Aly together. "I like that he's not her usual type. She tends to pick these super-smart, super-intense men who never make her happy."

"And you choose nice men you get bored with and slide into the friend category."

"That's not true." Joanna laughed. "Okay, that was the trajectory of my last few relationships, but the friend part was mutual."

"Um hum." She looked around the foyer. "So Bradford left?"

"Yep."

"Be careful with him, Joanna."

Here we go. "You, too? I'm sorry if you and Aly can't see what I see in him. I'm a grown woman. I don't need my friends' approval to decide if I like someone or not."

"Hey. Hey." Angelina put a hand up in appeal. "I'm not saying anything bad about Bradford. He has been a great friend to Connor. Under all that gruff talk there is a man who cares deeply about people. It's him I'm worried about. If you're not careful, you could break his heart."

Joanna's eyes rounded. "Me? What are you talking about? We're barely friends."

"Right and you're certain that's how he sees you as well."

"Hold on. Did Bradford say something?"

"Sure. He took me aside at recess and told me he's totally crushing on you but made me pinkie swear I wouldn't tell you. No. But I'm not blind. He couldn't take his eyes off you."

Joanna went back over their conversations in her head. "He's not interested in me. He keeps telling me to leave him alone." She chewed her bottom lip. "And most of the time we're talking about Dylan." Her mouth rounded. "If he does like me at all, that might be annoying."

"You think?" Angelina smacked herself in the forehead. "For someone who claims to be a great reader of men, you didn't read this one very well."

"Because I don't see Bradford that way." She saw him as someone who'd been hurt, someone on the outside looking in at a life he couldn't figure out how to access. She stopped when she remembered the connection she'd felt with him when they'd done the tequila shots. It had been a surprisingly sexy experience that had left her feeling confused. She'd expected to feel that way with Dylan. "I may have for a moment."

Bradford wasn't classically handsome the way Dylan was. His features were ruggedly imperfect. He had several scars on his face, some faint as if they'd been there a very long time, some more pronounced. The deepest was on the left side of his face, through his eyebrow and then curving across his cheek. Coupled with the little he had shared about his life, the scars spoke of painful times beyond what Joanna had ever known. She could picture him in her mind so easily. He did his best to conceal how he felt about most things, but there were tell signs. His eyes tended to narrow right before his mouth curled with a smile. His hands clenched and revealed when he was tense even when he kept his expression emotionless. She didn't know what to label how she felt about him, but there was something drawing her to him. Still, he'd spent most of the evening walking away from her. "He's not into me."

"How do you feel about him?"

Joanna didn't have an instant answer for that. "He's a tough person to get to know."

"But he's worth the effort."

"Isn't everyone?"

"Touché. I've probably said this all wrong, but we've been friends a long time. I know you're chasing Bradford with the best of intentions, but if you're not truly interested in him I'd give him space."

"I'm not chasing him."

"You bolted after him when he left the table."

"Because I felt bad about how Clay had essentially run him off."

"Exactly. You feel bad for him, but he's not one of your rescue horses. He might confuse your concern with more and that's where he'll get hurt."

Joanna frowned. "I—I—" She stopped and started over. "I don't want that. He does keep asking me to leave him alone."

Angelina hugged Joanna. "People tell us what they need."

Joanna's shoulders slumped. "I'm not handling things right tonight. Can I blame this damn gown? Not enough oxygen getting up to my brain? I can't breathe in it."

Angelina laughed. "Sure. Hey, you didn't do anything wrong. Maybe I shouldn't have said anything. I just care about you and him."

Joanna nodded. "Let's head back in." Just before they got to the door, she stopped. "Thanks Angelina. The last thing I want to do is hurt Bradford."

"I know. You're just too damn cute for your own good. Men get a little stupid around you."

"Me?" Joanna shook her head. "I had to buy a whole new set of jeans recently because my 'fat' jeans wouldn't snap."

"And yet, somehow you still fit through the ballroom doors. Women don't have to be a size zero to be attractive. There's a reason Dylan held you up as his fake girlfriend. You're beautiful, Joanna, on the inside as well as the outside."

Joanna smiled and hugged her friend. "I love you."

"Love you too. Now let's get back in there because the sharks are circling Dylan."

Laughing, Joanna said, "They can't have him since we've already decided he's Aly's."

Angelina laughed along. "Should we take what he wants into consideration?"

"Nah," they said at the same time then shared another laugh.

Back at the table, Joanna took a seat between the tense-looking duo of Aly and Dylan. With relief, Dylan said, "Joanna, I need to mingle. Come with me?"

After exchanging a look with Angelina, Joanna made a face and bent to touch her lower calf. "I would, but I twisted my ankle out in the foyer and I should probably stay off it."

Aly's expression was instantly concerned. "How bad is it?

Is it swelling already? You should ice it. Want me to ask our server to bring you some?"

Joanna tucked the ankle in question behind her other. "No need. It'll be fine. Barely twisted it at all. I just don't want to tempt fate and wobble around on these heels. Why don't you go with Dylan?"

Aly and Dylan appeared equally at a loss for what to say.

Clay interjected. "Nothing shocking about a movie star attending an event with two beautiful women."

"True enough," Dylan said with a nod.

Aly rolled her eyes. "Thanks, but I'll pass."

Leaning forward to talk around Joanna, Dylan said, "You should wait until you're actually asked before you turn a man down."

Aly mumbled, "Rude."

"There you go," Dylan said, "getting all judgy again."

Aly sputtered.

Dylan stood. "This has been great. Connor, I'll call you tomorrow. Clay, I'll set up everything with the production team so you'll all have VIP treatment on set. Joanna, thank you for playing the role of my fake date long enough for me to hang out." He stepped closer to Aly, bent, and said something to her.

She glared at him and turned away.

Joanna was about to ask her what Dylan had said when Clay slid into the seat Dylan had just vacated.

"Joanna."

She turned slowly toward him. "Yes, Clay?"

"I believe you require my services."

Her eyes widened. "And those would be?"

He handed her a white card with gold lettering. All it said was: Fairy Godfather Extraordinaire.

Joanna turned the card over. "I—thank you. I couldn't."

"It's overwhelmingly generous on my part, I know, but I like you." Clay adjusted his already perfect tie.

Although it had been fun to imagine what it would be like to be the recipient of a little of Clay's magic, she was no longer interested in Dylan. "It certainly is a generous offer."

Aly sighed. "I hope your services include lessons in fidelity, because I don't see Dylan settling for one woman any time soon."

"I'm not interested in Dylan that way," Joanna said.

Aly's eyes narrowed and she lowered her voice. "Since when?"

Joanna glanced around the table. All eyes were on her and ears perked to their conversation. She considered lying and saying, "Since always," but these were her friends. Most of them, anyway. She wasn't sure what to think of Clay and Lexi yet and Daphne was sweet but still an unknown. "Since I agreed to a fake date with him and realized I didn't want it to become real. He's great, we just don't have that zing."

"Zing," Clay repeated. "Lexi, hear that, she's a romantic? This is definitely going to work."

Lexi chimed in, "I want to disagree, Clay, but I think you're right. She'd be perfect for him."

"Perfect for who?" Connor asked.

"Whom." Clay dusted imaginary lint off his shoulder. "And Bradford."

Connor's face lit up. "Are they a thing? Joanna, have you been holding out on us? That's fantastic."

"And unexpected," Daphne said in a low tone.

Joanna's head spun toward Daphne. For just a second she looked neither shy nor afraid—instead the look in her eyes was . . . cunning? The thought gave Joanna an uneasy feeling. Daphne ducked her head and seemed embarrassed, Joanna decided she'd misread Daphne's expression. "As well as not happening. Bradford and I are friends. That's it. And we're barely that."

"Not for long," Clay said with confidence. "Not if I have anything to do with it."

Joanna met Angelina's gaze across the table. She'd meant what she said earlier about not wanting to hurt Bradford and that included embarrassing him. She was sure he wouldn't appreciate being the topic of discussion in his absence. She placed the card on the table. "I am so honored that you would consider helping me out, Clay, but I must decline. Thank you, though."

Clay looked from the card on the table then back at Joanna. "Connor, tell her what you said to me at first."

"I said no?" Connor said with an awkward smile.

"You even called Dax because you thought he could influence me one way or another."

"I did." Connor put an arm around Angelina's shoulders. "When something is meant to be it doesn't need help."

"Oh, I helped." Clay started counting off on his fingers. "Who advised you to play hard to get?"

Angelina laughed up at Connor. "Is that what you were

doing?"

Connor shrugged, but his face was red. "I tried."

"Who put you in charge of his Gold Star initiative so you could hire Angelina?" Clay continued.

"Hey, I've busted my ass for the organization," Connor protested.

"You absolutely have," Clay agreed, "but admit that it gave you a way to spend time together."

Angelina hugged Connor while smiling at Clay. "However it happened, I'm grateful it did."

After giving her a quick kiss on the lips, Connor said, "So am I. The how doesn't matter." He turned to Clay and grinned. "I'm glad you didn't listen to me."

Clay looked Joanna right in the eye. "I'm sorry, I had a hard time hearing you. What did you say, Connor?"

Lexi shook her head but she was laughing. "Oh, Clay. Do you know how fun you are to watch in action?"

"Don't mess with my game head, Lexi. I'm one for one. I can't mess this up."

"One for one." Lexi winked at Joanna. "He helped one couple get together. I'd hate to mess with a solid record like that. Joanna you have to give Clay a chance to prove himself."

The puppy-dog look Clay gave Joanna was confusing. Why would such a powerful man care about her love life? "This is all a game to you, isn't it?"

His smile was easy. "Of course it is, but when I play everyone wins."

Joanna looked from Angelina who seemed cautiously

optimistic to Aly who appeared skeptical, but that was nothing new. Joanna picked up the white card again and weighed the possibilities. "We'd have to agree to some ground rules."

Clay sat back and tapped his fingers on the table. "What do you think, Lexi? Does Cinderella get to set conditions?"

Laying her hand over her husband's, Lexi said, "Always."

He nodded then turned back to Joanna. "This is already better—Connor fought me all the way. Sweet Joanna, tell me these rules of yours."

Joanna's chin rose. "None of this is ever used to embarrass Bradford."

Clay had the grace to look a little chastened. "Agreed."

"Also, if it turns out that he and I don't have a connection—you promise to find him someone who will bring a smile back to his face."

The table fell silent for a moment.

Clay blinked a few times then cleared his throat. "Wow, you got me with that last one. I can do that."

"Me too," Connor said from across the table. "If it doesn't work out with Bradford, reconsider Dylan. He needs someone like you. He's putting on a big show here, but he's missing us and there's a lot he's still figuring out."

Aly looked around the room as if seeking Dylan out in the crowd. He was once again surrounded by female admirers. She shook her head and looked away. "I'm sure he'll find a way to ease his pain."

Joanna elbowed her. *I know you're scared, Aly, but knock it off.*

Clay waved a hand in the air. "Back to Bradford. We need to find a way for you to spend time together."

"That might be harder than you think," Joanna said. "I asked him if he wanted to get breakfast with me tomorrow and/or go for a walk and he said no to both." On Clay's prompting she shared the details of where and when she'd asked him to meet her.

Clay looked to his wife. "Lexi, are you thinking what I'm thinking?"

"Yep. He'll definitely be there." Lexi smiled.

"So I should plan like he's meeting me?" Joanna asked.

"No," Clay said. "I'll plan like he's meeting you. You just show up."

Letting Clay get involved was a crazy idea.

There were so many ways it could go wrong.

Still, Joanna believed in fate and things working out the way they were supposed to. Maybe all she was meant to do was come into Bradford's life to remind him that people cared about him. Or maybe they were meant for more.

Either way, she was drawn to him in a way that could not be ignored. She'd never been afraid to follow her heart and right then it was telling her that Bradford needed her. How? She wasn't sure, but she couldn't walk away.

"Okay. I'm in."

Chapter Five

A LITTLE AFTER three in the morning Bradford woke in a full sweat and sat straight up in his bed. His breathing was ragged, his muscles were shaking. He rubbed his hands over his face and swore.

He never remembered his dreams, and that was a gift. During the day he normally had tight control over where his thoughts went, but at night his subconscious fed him all kinds of shit that shook him to the core. He often woke with a deep sense of dread and remorse.

Throwing back the blanket, Bradford flipped on the light and walked his naked ass to his closet. With sleep an impossibility, he donned shorts and a T-shirt and headed out for a run.

Exercise always cleared his head. He ran until the weight of his dreams fell away. He kept running until the endorphins kicked in and he felt strong enough to fight back his demons.

He couldn't outrun images of Joanna or get her invitation out of his head. He knew all the reasons why he shouldn't meet her that morning, but he wanted to.

That was the real problem.

She's not interested in me.

She has her sight set on Dylan.

Seeing her again would be a waste of my time and hers. I'm not looking for friendship from her and she's not looking for more than that from me.

So why the fuck can't I get her out of my head?

On his way back to his New York apartment, he hit the gym for a heavy workout. She was there in his thoughts regardless of how hard he pushed himself. After they'd spoken, had she returned to the table and asked Dylan to breakfast?

Had they hooked up?

Is he fucking her right now?

He didn't want to know. Knowledge was power, and normally he made it his business to know everything about everyone—but she was scrambling his brain.

Beneath the hot spray of the shower he imagined a different ending to his tequila lesson—one that included him kissing the salt off her lips and tasting the mixture of her and the liquor. He hated how easy it was to imagine her hands on him and the sounds she might make as he brought her pleasure.

With only a towel draped around his waist he paced his apartment. He told himself the only sensible thing to do was to put some distance between Joanna and himself. There was always work for someone like him. Somewhere in the world someone was in peril. The more dangerous the mission, the better.

He picked up his phone to arrange for just such a job, but instead reread Joanna's texts to him. He'd outright told her he wouldn't be at breakfast. Her answer? "That's okay, I will be."

No one was that fucking easygoing.

She'd said it, but there was zero chance she meant it.

He imagined her sitting at a table with a swear jar she'd decorated for him—waiting for him. *Yeah, like that's fucking reality.*

He tossed his phone down on his bed and headed into his closet to choose an outfit. He caught a glimpse of himself in a full-length mirror and stopped. Each scar on his chest had a story behind it—some he wasn't proud of. He shifted in the mirror so he could see the back of his left shoulder that still bore the marks of the chain whipping he'd received when he'd tried to save his sister. He raised a hand and traced the largest scar on his cheek. The slice had been delivered with a broken beer bottle and meant for his neck. The man who'd given it to him was the one who'd initially brought Ella back into the gang.

His death had been swifter than he deserved.

Bradford turned away from the mirror. His outer body was impressively damaged, but his insides were a hundred times uglier. Although he'd never hurt an innocent, he'd spent most of his life rescuing them from people who were just as fucked up as he was.

As he dressed in jeans and a T-shirt, he told himself it was better for people like him to stay with their own kind. All he'd do was disappoint Joanna and all she'd do was remind him of everything he wasn't.

If she's stupid enough to sit in a restaurant waiting for someone who said they wouldn't be there—that's on her.

He walked back into his bedroom to retrieve his phone and paused. If she actually did go to breakfast alone, did that mean she'd also take a walk around the pond by herself?

He didn't know the area. Were the paths there heavily traveled? Had there been violent incidents in the area recently? *I should have researched the place.*

I never fly blind.

I'm losing my focus.

He exceeded the speed limit the entire way to the restaurant, another out-of-character act. His work required staying under the radar—invisible. No one did what he did without accumulating enemies.

Another reason not to get involved with Joanna. For people like him, caring about anyone gave those who would want to hurt him the ability to do so. *Been there. Done that. Not signing up for that ride again.*

Her car was there. Was she alone?

He parked a distance away but didn't immediately get out.

If she was with someone, there was no need for her to know he was there. If she was alone, he could keep things casual. *I'll go in, make sure she's safe, leave.*

He was walking toward the entrance of the restaurant when she came out the door. She looked disappointed, but her head was held high. When he moved her eyes flew to his and the smile that spread across her face knocked his breath clear out of him. He swayed on his feet. *Holy shit.*

She was before him in a heartbeat. "You came."

He took a deep breath. He wanted to ask her if she was alone. If she wasn't he wanted to haul her out of there and show her why he was the better choice. *But I'm not.*

She dug into her oversized purse and produced a gift-wrapped box. "I brought this for you."

He didn't reach for it. That was too dangerous. Being with her was as jolting as stepping out into bright sunlight after spending a lifetime in darkness. She was too much—too happy, too tempting. He ached in a way that was terrifying . . . *and fucking incredible.* "I didn't like the idea of you here alone."

She tossed the gift at him.

He caught it.

"Open it."

"No need." He shook the box. "It's loose coins in a glass jar I'll never use."

"I guess it's not a surprise since I told you what I'd bring you." Laughter lit her eyes. "I added a few coins because the way you swear I thought you might need some help covering the cost. Isn't that what friends are for?"

He leaned down until his mouth hovered over hers. It would have been so easy to give in to the desire pulsing through him. His mind was full of X-rated things friends could do together, but he kept all of those thoughts to himself and straightened. He forced his attention back to the gift in his hand. "I have all—"

With a wave of her hand she cut him off. "I know. I

know. You have all the friends you need. But you're here, so I know you care."

She had him there. "I couldn't let you walk around in the woods on your own."

"Because you care."

He wasn't going there. Instead he shook the box again. "Who even has change anymore?"

She laughed. "Open the damn gift."

He did and pulled out a mason jar with a large white label on one side. He started to read it, a smile spreading across his face as he did. "Swearing fees: Said in pain: 25 cents, Said in anger: $10, Said in ecstasy: no charge."

She looked so proud of herself. "I was shooting for cute and a little sexy."

She'd hit her mark, too easily for his comfort. He replaced the jar in the box and held it out for her to take back. "I'd give it to Dylan if I were you."

"You're not me." She folded her arms across her chest. "I always say thank you when someone takes the time to make a gift for me."

His hand clenched on the box as he lowered it to his side. "You're playing a dangerous game."

She searched his face. "You're wrong. I don't play games." She uncrossed her arms. "I'm not interested in Dylan. He was a fun idea, but he's not my type."

"Don't." The words were wrenched out of Bradford.

She frowned. "I like you. I don't know if this has the potential to go anywhere, but I'd like to get to know you. Maybe we'll go for a walk together and discover we have nothing in common and no reason to meet up again. Or maybe we'll decide different isn't bad."

His chest tightened and anger bubbled within him. "Different." His laugh held only dark humor. "You have no fucking idea."

Without missing a beat, she said, "Ten dollars."

"What?"

"You heard me." They stood there looking at each other in a silent standoff.

His unexplainable anger began to subside. There were two clear paths before him and his response to her soft reprimand would be a step down one or the other. He could hand the jar back to her and tell her he had no intention of changing for anyone. Or . . .

He dug his wallet out of his back pocket, withdrew a ten-dollar bill and stuffed it through the slit on the top of the jar. There was no triumph in her expression, no sign of gloating. When he looked in her eyes he saw only the friendship she kept offering him.

She claimed to like him.

The tone of the gift implied she also found him attractive.

There probably were instances where differences were good, but this was not one of them. He told himself to walk away, but he couldn't get himself to.

Her smile sent a wave of warmth through him. She referenced the building behind her. "There's an hour wait inside or I'd suggest we get something to eat. Instead, why don't you put the gift in your car and we can go for that walk?"

He nodded then started walking with her in the direction of his car. He unlocked the side door, opened it, then after placing the box in the back, he said, "Thank you for the gift."

"You're welcome."

After closing the door of his car, he turned and discovered her so close to him his breath caught in his throat. She needed to know who she was dealing with. "I've done a lot of things in my life I'm not proud of."

She held his gaze. "Have you ever killed anyone?"

"Yes, but no one the world isn't better without." With a self-deprecating smile, he added, "And I'm seriously trying to cut down."

She let out a shaky breath. "I can't tell if you're joking."

"I wish I were." He leaned in. "I'm too far gone, Joanna. You can't bring someone like me back to where you are." He straightened. "There's too much blood on my hands."

She wrapped her arms around her waist. "How many?"

She didn't want to know and he didn't want to say, so he didn't.

After a moment, she said, "Tell me about one. Any one."

He shook his head.

"Not the details," she pressed, "the reason. One person. One reason."

Everything he did was highly classified and even Ian didn't know all of it. Telling her anything made no sense at all, but he said, "A recent one kidnapped a senator's daughter. I'm attempting to work with law enforcement more, but some situations are best handled with swift precision. He was a repeat offender. His first victim was taken in Spain. The family paid the ransom but never got the child back. His first kidnapping was practice for the big target—the big payout. He had no intention of releasing the senator's daughter or negotiating."

"You saved a child," she said in a low tone.

"Don't pretty it up. I'm a cold-blooded killer. No remorse. No mercy. I'm only scared when I enjoy it."

She rubbed her hands up and down her upper arms as if fighting off a chill. "Do you? Enjoy it?"

He looked away. "Sometimes. When I take aim and I can see their victim's face in my head, when I know exactly what happened to them at the hands of my target. Sometimes it feels good in that moment." He met her gaze, letting her see the darkness in him. "But every kill is a mark on my soul. There are days when I don't see the difference between who I am and who I'm sent to take down."

She swallowed visibly. "Do you work for the CIA or FBI or any of the alphabets?"

He almost smiled. She was scared, but wasn't running. "I'm the one they call when things get—complicated."

She nodded slowly. "Ian used to work with you."

"Yes, but now he has a desk job."

"Did he also—?"

She didn't finish the question he wouldn't have been able to answer anyway. They fell into a long silence. A mother with children came out of the restaurant and went to the car beside Bradford's. While she was securing a toddler into a car seat, her slightly older child bolted, crashed into Bradford's legs, and fell backward. He caught the boy before he hit the ground and righted him. "Easy there."

The boy's bottom lip quivered, likely from the scare of almost getting hurt. "You've got a big boo boo on your face."

The mother sprinted to her son's side and scooped him up. "I'm so sorry."

"Not a problem," Bradford said. He winked at the woman then touched the scar on his cheek. "Boo boos happen when you're not careful. You should stay with your mom. Parking lots are dangerous. Cars can't see little ones."

The little boy hugged his mother's neck and nodded. "Boo boos hurt."

"They sure do," Bradford agreed.

After the car pulled away, Bradford turned his attention back to Joanna.

She was looking at him with an expression in her eyes that only made him hate himself more. She stepped closer and laid her hand on his scarred cheek. "I'm so sorry for the things you've seen and the things you've been asked to do. I can't imagine the price you pay for the good you've done."

"Don't fucking pity me."

"Ten dollars."

JOANNA FELT COMPASSION for him, not pity. Although she hadn't grown up with money, she had been raised to believe in community and responsibility. Her father often said a person's character was revealed in how they treated the vulnerable. There was real despair and self-hatred in his eyes and it broke her heart.

The hair on the back of her neck had stood up when he'd admitted he sometimes enjoyed ending someone's life. When he'd explained why though, she'd been reminded of stories her grandmother had told her about her grandfather after she'd had a few cups of moonshine. He'd been drafted right out of college, even though the government had claimed that wasn't their policy. He'd been sent to fight in the front lines of a war he'd done nothing to create and had been powerless to end. Her grandmother said he'd fought like a hero only to come home to be spit on by the public.

Although she'd never met her grandfather, long afternoons with moonshine and her grandmother had given her a pretty good idea of how haunted he'd been by what he'd seen and done. Her grandmother had once said, "The line between heaven and hell blurs, Joanna, when good people are asked to do heinous things to save others."

It took time for Joanna to understand what that meant, but the more she'd learned about her grandfather the more she understood why he'd taken his own life. She didn't agree with his decision, but she understood that the choices he'd made weighed on him and that weight had eventually been too heavy for him.

My parents would have never let Grandma watch me had they known how much she shared with me. The night before her grandfather had taken his own life he'd confessed something to her grandmother that her grandmother had confessed to Joanna on her own deathbed. During his last tour he'd caught two men from his unit playing poker with the stakes being a young girl who was sitting there terrified.

Her grandmother told her he'd tried to get them to do the right thing, even threatened to expose them if they didn't. They said they would kill the girl and anyone else they wanted and that blood would be on his hands because he'd made it so they couldn't release them. Her grandfather killed those two men and released the girl.

The deaths of those two men had been blamed on an attack that happened early the next morning, an attack that took out everyone in his company except him. He'd been injured, but alive. Had his life been spared because he'd spared the girl's? Had releasing her cost the lives of everyone in his company?

He was never the same after that night. Was he a hero? Was he a killer? A traitor? Her grandmother said he suffered a breakdown after that incident and that was why he was discharged. He lived a quiet life for many years, long enough to raise a family and be a good husband, but he'd never conquered the shame and self-loathing.

When she looked into Bradford's eyes she saw a pain she understood. *Grandma would have liked Bradford.*

Bradford shifted beneath the sustained silence from Joanna. He opened the car door, took out his wallet, pulled out a stack of twenties and stuffed them in the jar.

It was comical, but Joanna fought back a smile. "That's not the way the jar works."

He slammed the door of his car shut. "It is now."

She did smile at that one, then her expression turned serious. "What you think is pity is actually compassion. I don't know what you've been through, or what you've done, but if you did it to save others—you're a hero in my book."

He leaned back against his car. "I'm no hero."

She didn't doubt that he believed that about himself. "Let's go for a walk."

In a strangled voice, he asked, "Why aren't you fucking running from me?"

She held his gaze. "Would you ever hurt me?"

"Never."

"Then let's go for that walk. I have a story I think you should hear."

He pushed off his car and glared down at her, but she was beginning to think all of that anger was directed at himself, not her. When she held out her hand to him he looked down at it and froze.

There was no encouragement in his body language, but she had to believe their paths had crossed for a reason. *He needs to know he's not alone.* She continued to hold out her hand to him.

For a long moment he neither moved nor said anything, then he laced his fingers with hers. "You're trouble, Joanna Ervin."

"So I've heard." She pulled him until he fell into step beside her. They started down a path along the edge of the pond. A couple going in the opposite direction passed them, but once they were alone again Joanna started to tell Bradford about her grandfather.

His hand tightened painfully on hers when she told him about the night that had forever changed her grandfather. He didn't say anything though, and she took that as encouragement. "After both of his children were out of the house and he thought my grandmother could survive on her own, he confessed everything to her then took his own life."

Bradford's expression was tight. "I can understand that."

She pulled him to a stop. "I can't. I feel cheated that I never got to meet him."

Bradford nodded.

She continued, "For me, the saddest part is that my grandfather died thinking he was a traitor—a murderer. And after he died my grandmother carried his guilt and shame until cancer took her from us. I'm not ashamed of what he did. He chose humanity and mercy."

"And would have rotted in prison for it had his secret been exposed."

"Probably, but it wasn't. He couldn't have known that sparing her would get his company killed."

Bradford shook his head. "He should have. It was common for the enemy to use their children as scouts and weapons."

Real sadness swept through Joanna. "How could anyone tell an enemy from an innocent in that war?"

"You couldn't."

"So, was he right? Was he wrong?"

"It's not for me to stand in judgment."

"What would you have done?"

"I would have fucking killed those men."

They began to walk again, hand in hand, without speaking. "I hate that my grandfather didn't believe my grandmother could handle the truth about him. He wasn't as alone as he felt."

"He wanted to protect her."

"But he left her. That didn't protect her. She could have stood by him and helped him conquer those demons if she'd known what he was fighting. Connor says part of the Gold Star initiative he runs for Clay includes mental health services for veterans who make it back, but need mental health support. A soldier's pain ripples through whole families."

"I'm not a soldier."

"But—aren't you? You might not wear a uniform, but if you're risking your life to save innocents . . . do you need a label?"

"You don't know the things I've done."

"So tell me."

He shook his head.

She yanked him to a stop. "Because you think I can't handle it? Or because you don't trust me with the truth?"

"A little of both."

She released his hand. "I can't make you trust me, but I'm stronger than I appear. If you really are the person you say you are, your secrets won't crush me—or endanger you. I could be wrong, but I have to believe my grandfather wouldn't have taken his own life if he'd trusted someone with his secrets earlier. You don't have to tell me, but you should tell someone."

They walked on, greeting another couple who passed, before stopping on a small bridge that crossed a cement dam. He gripped the railing with both hands. "I told you about my parents, but I also lost my sister."

In a monotone voice he told her about how he and his sister had been separated after his parents' death. He told her about how she'd returned to the streets, joined the gang his parents had belonged to, and what an ugly path that had led her down.

Joanna was fighting back tears when he described the beating that had nearly killed him and how ultimately, regardless of how he'd fought for her, he'd lost her to an overdose. She hugged her arms around herself when he coldly described how he'd hunted down those responsible for her death and eliminated them.

After a short silence, she asked, "How did you meet Ian?"

He told her about joining the Army and the kidnapped schoolgirls both he and Ian had set out to save. "We've worked together ever since." He laughed without humor. "Well, until he met Claire."

There was no reason for Bradford to lie, and his story fit with everything she knew about Ian and his change in careers. It was also too reminiscent of what her grandfather had done for her to believe she'd met Bradford by chance. "What kind of missions did you and Ian go on?"

He told her about several, including the one with the Somalian pirates that convinced Ian he couldn't continue that lifestyle and have a family. "Ian understood that he had to choose. Caring about anyone while doing what we do is a liability."

"Because?"

"Someone could use you against me."

That gave her arms goose bumps that she rubbed away with her hands. "So you could never have a normal life."

"That about sums it up."

"But Ian can?"

"Ian has me watching his back."

"Doesn't he watch yours?"

"You don't understand."

She didn't, but she had a feeling he wasn't being entirely honest. "I do. You're scared."

He spun on his heel toward her. "Don't go there."

"It's okay to be afraid. You've lost people you loved. It's natural to want to protect yourself from that kind of hurt again. It's just sad because you're the one writing the rules that hold you back."

His hands clenched at his sides. "I'm not afraid."

"I get that it's scary to even admit it."

He rubbed his hands over his face. A deep growl emanated from deep in his chest. "Fine. I'm a fucking mess on the inside. I don't care about anyone because I've seen what happens when I do. I refuse to give anyone that power over me again."

His words ripped through Joanna. She felt his pain so deeply it might have been her own. "Then they win."

"What?"

"Ultimately, those two horrible soldiers my grandfather killed won because they stole his ability to see the value of his own life. He gave them the ultimate win when he killed himself. You're doing the same."

He leaned down and growled in her face. "Don't pretend

you fucking know anything about me or what I'm doing with my life."

She raised her chin. "If your goal is to scare me, you won't. You know what scares me? The people you remove from the planet. Cold-blooded criminals. Especially those who go after the weak. I don't understand cruelty simply for the sake of being cruel. I am constantly shocked by the violence and hatred people spew toward each other, especially when they feel they can get away with it. I can barely watch the news each night because humanity scares the shit out of me. But you? You're sad and angry. Were all the choices you made right? I'm sure they weren't, but there is no absolute right or wrong. That's a lie they tell us as children. Good or bad, hero or traitor, it's never as simple as one or the other. That's what makes life messy. So swear— yell—let that anger out on me, but know that when you do . . . you lose and they win."

She started walking, leaving him to either choose to stay behind or follow her.

Chapter Six

*G*O.
*I don't need you or your motivational speeches.
My life is fine just the way it is.*

The farther she walked from him, the more he questioned the stance he was taking. He hated his life. Hated himself. Nothing brought him joy. Nothing seemed to matter anymore.

Except her.

He took a slow step after her then lengthened his stride. When she disappeared from view, he broke into a sprint. Rounding a bend in the path, he caught up to her. She smiled at him as if he hadn't just sworn at her and she hadn't just walked away from him.

He fell into step beside her. This was uncharted territory for him. "I'm sorry."

"Me too." She offered her hand again. His heart raced in his chest as he took it back in his. "I asked some tough questions. Thank you for being honest."

They walked in silence for a while. He'd never been as aware of another human being as he was of her. His senses were not only in overdrive but exclusively focused on her. He loved the way she glanced at him then away again. She had no problem leading when the path narrowed, and he was perfectly happy following.

"Is there anything you'd like to ask about me?" she asked.

"Can't imagine there's much I don't already know."

She paused. "Really?"

"It's common for me to do a background check on anyone I know will be in the mix."

They started walking again. "A background check. Sounds serious. So, somewhere there's a file on me."

He tapped one side of his temple. "I don't write things down."

"Right. Less evidence."

"You catch on quick."

"How do you gather information? Social media? Or do you hunt around for information like they do on detective shows?"

"Depends on what I need to know about someone."

She stopped and turned toward him. "Me. How did you gather information about me?"

He shifted from one foot to the other. "You were a special case."

"A special case?" Her eyes lit with interest. "Why?"

"Because no one is as perfect as you seem. I was sure you were hiding something."

"Wow. Okay. What did you uncover?"

A corner of his mouth twitched with a smile he held

back. "You're either a boring fuck or you choose men who are."

Her mouth rounded and she yanked on his hand. "I didn't see that one coming. For your information, I'm far from boring in bed."

"I'll take your word for it." He liked how easy it was to rile her, and she looked adorably flustered.

She released his hand and poked a finger into his chest. "If you're ever lucky enough to be with me I'll prove it to you."

He laughed and wrapped his hand around hers. "Promises. Promises."

She pursed her lips and pulled her hand free. "Why would you think I'm bad in bed?"

"It might not have been you, but you barely had sex with your last boyfriend."

"How would you know how much we did or didn't have?"

"He told me."

Her hands went to her hips and she did not look happy. He was beginning to think he might have overestimated the humor in this for her. She said, "Well so much for not kissing and telling. No, I don't believe he would have told you anything. Rob and I ended things on a good note."

"He was pretty shit-faced at the time."

Her eyes narrowed. "You got him drunk so you could ask him questions about me?"

He held her gaze and shrugged.

She looked about to tell him what she thought about

that, then her expression softened. "You asked my ex about me because you like me."

"I told you, it's my business to know everything about who I'm dealing with."

She smiled. "And that includes drinking with their exes? I call bullshit."

She was good. "I may have inquired into your background more than most."

"Because you like me."

He leaned down and growled into her ear. "Because I can't get you out of my head."

She shivered and her eyes half closed. He almost kissed her then. He wanted to. She wanted it as well. He held back only because he heard voices coming down the path toward them. In a husky tone, she asked, "What would your ex-girlfriends say about you?"

"Nothing," he said while tracing her jaw with his thumb. "I don't date."

She tipped her head to one side. "Isn't that—frustrating?"

He chuckled. "I never said I'm not having sex. I just don't do the whole 'see you tomorrow' thing."

"One-night stands only."

"Nothing wrong with variety." She was definitely judging his lifestyle, but in that area, at least, he'd never done anything he was ashamed of. He liked sex. The women he hooked up with had a good time while they were with him. No strings. No promises. No regrets.

She stepped back. "I couldn't do that."

"You'd rather date men you don't want to fuck."

"Not that I owe you an explanation, but I'll admit I have chosen a few who would have been better off left in the friend category."

He gripped her chin and tipped it upward. "I don't want to be your friend."

She licked her bottom lip. "Then don't bore me in bed."

He laughed once, released her chin, then laughed again. She constantly surprised him, but in the best ways. "Okay."

"Okay." She straightened her clothing.

It felt completely natural to hold out a hand for her to take. She laced her fingers through his just as a group of teenagers walked by. "I was wrong."

They started walking down the path side by side again. "About?"

"There's a lot I don't know about you—but I want to."

A huge smile spread across her face. "That's the nicest thing you've ever said to me."

The women he'd chosen in the past enjoyed his bad-boy image. None had ever pushed him for more or tried to rein him in. What was he doing with a woman who did? "No one has ever accused me of being nice."

Her hand tightened on his. "Then they must not have taken the time to get to know you."

They rounded a corner that opened up to a field nearly filled with a huge white tent. A sign beside it read: PRIVATE EVENT.

A man in a white tuxedo waved to them to come over.

"What the fuck is that?" Bradford asked.

Joanna cringed. "There's something I should probably tell you."

Bradford tensed. He lived in a way that ensured there was very little he didn't see coming. Joanna was clouding his judgment and this was more evidence of that. He had no idea the large tent would be there, who was involved in assembling it, or its purpose. Not knowing was sloppy and was how men like him got themselves and the people they cared about killed. "What don't I know?"

She made another pained face then released his hand and dug through her purse. A moment later she held up a white business card with gold lettering. He read it and swore. Her gaze fell and he swore again. She stuffed the card back in her bag. "I should have said no."

"You should have." Irritation with Clay battled with concern for Joanna. "I did."

"He asked you too?" Her shoulders rose and fell in an awkward move. "I didn't know that. I'm sorry."

He almost swore again but held it back. She probably had no idea what a royal pain in the ass Clay could be. If he thought it wouldn't probably kill Clay, he'd give the man one good punch to the head as a reminder of what happens to people who meddle in other people's lives for entertainment. "Don't be sorry; this is classic Clay. He failed with me so he went for an easier target."

"Wow. Do you actually listen to what you say? Play that last part back in your head and imagine you're me."

He did. *Shit.* "I didn't mean it that way."

She flexed her shoulders and held his gaze. "I know.

That's why I'm giving you a chance to say it differently."

He groaned. "Clay likes to fuck with me. I'm not happy that this time he used you to do it."

"Better." She adjusted her purse on her shoulder. "I don't know your history with Clay, and I've seen his lack of tact when it comes to dealing with you, but I do believe he likes you."

"I don't care how he feels about anything as long as it doesn't affect my life."

She looked over at the tent then back at Bradford. "You aren't curious at all?"

He shook his head. "Not in the least."

She sighed. "That's a shame, because I am." Her attention returned to the large white tent. "I've never had a fairy godfather. I certainly never had anyone surprise me with something like this. I need to know what's inside."

"You're going to make me go inside with you, aren't you?"

"Not at all." She gave him a long look. "You're a smart man. I'm sure you can find the way back to your car if you want to."

Bradford folded his arms across his chest. "It won't stop here. If you give Clay any encouragement at all there's no way he won't come back with something bigger and crazier. This is a game to him."

She smiled. "I know, but where's your sense of adventure? Of fun? Do you think Clay has any desire to see either of us hurt?"

Grudgingly, he admitted, "No."

"So, what are you afraid of? That you might enjoy yourself?" She took a step toward the tent.

"For all we know he has hidden cameras in there."

She took another step toward the tent. "All he'll see is me smiling and laughing because I love surprises, and I bet this one is fun."

Bradford closed the distance between them. He stopped within inches of her and hovered without touching. "I don't like surprises."

She touched the scarred side of his face gently. "I understand why, but I'd like to share this with you. If it's annoying, we run out together. If it's fun, we'll have a great shared memory."

He didn't walk into a room without knowing who would be there and what their vulnerabilities were. She was asking him to blindly follow her into an unknown—go against everything experience had taught him to do. The contents of the tent didn't scare him, but the lure of her did. He would have said he couldn't be manipulated, but all she had to do was look up at him with those big eyes and that gorgeous smile and there was nothing he could deny her. "Okay."

"Yes!" A huge smile lit her face and she went up on her toes and kissed his cheek. He closed his eyes as emotion and desire rocked through him.

Her hand closed around his and she tugged him to follow her.

He was tempted to pull her into his arms and kiss her until she completely forgot about anything but finding a much more private place where they could enjoy each other.

Instead, he smiled back at her and matched his pace to hers.

Fucking Clay.

For your sake, you'd better have brought your best fairy god-father game today.

SOMETIMES YOU JUST *have to trust your gut.*

And people.

That's what Joanna told herself as she and Bradford approached the man in the white tux who greeted them with a formal nod and, "Miss Ervin. Mr. Wilson. Welcome."

"And if that's not who we are?" Bradford asked.

The man took out his phone and turned the screen toward them revealing a photograph of the two of them. "Then Mr. Landon has friends who are your doppelgangers."

Bradford arched an eyebrow.

Joanna leaned closer to see the photo. It was taken the night before just after he'd walked away from the table and she'd chased after him. Her hands were on her hips and he was looking down at her. She cringed at the amount of cleavage she hadn't realized her gown had shown, but then took note of the flush of his cheeks. *He's definitely into me. How did I not see that?*

Desire fluttered through her. How was it possible to feel such a strong connection to him before they'd even kissed? She'd joked that the way to keep her was to not bore her in bed, but she was beginning to think it was more complicated than that. They exchanged a look that confirmed he could get her heart racing and her body craving his without so much as a touch. How hot would that flame burn when they actually fanned it?

She tore her attention from him and forced herself to respond to the man in the tux. "That's us."

The man repocketed his phone then clapped his hands and the flap at the front of the tent was pulled back. "Then welcome to the Glass Slipper."

Bradford groaned.

Joanna stood straighter and looked him in the eye. "You don't have to come in, but if you do, please don't ruin it for me."

He took a moment to answer, then said, "Understood." The smile he gave her looked a little forced, but she accepted his attempt.

Together they stepped through the opening of the tent and into a small area that was portioned off from the rest. The part they entered had one round glass table set for two with white frosted plates and silverware. The seat the man in the tux held out for Joanna was clear acrylic. From the white and gold pattern of the flooring to the twinkling crystal pumpkins hanging from a chandelier, the setting was magical.

Joanna sat down with wide eyes and a huge smile.

Bradford sat across from her. "Wow, this is tacky."

Some of the wind went out of Joanna's sails. She was tired of trying to get him to see the fun in it. Maybe they were too different.

The silence that followed was uncomfortably long. He drummed his fingers on the table. She told herself it was okay when reality didn't live up to fantasy.

Another man in a white tux appeared and handed them both a menu with a few choices, some labeled as vegetarian friendly. Clay was a considerate fairy godfather. She wasn't sure how he knew, but she'd have to remember to thank him.

Bradford read his menu then laid it down and growled, "Are you wishing you were here with someone else?"

His question took her by surprise. She put her menu down as well and chose her words carefully. "I'm wondering if we have what it takes to get beyond how different we are, but there isn't anyone I'd rather be here with. I just wish you could let go and see it the way I do."

He looked away then back at her. "Tell me how you see all this."

His reply didn't feel like a challenge as much as a sincere request. She waved a hand at the chandelier. "Look at the crystal pumpkins. I have no idea where Clay would have found something like that, but it took effort on his part to think this up. It does border on tacky . . . but it's also unique and playful and thoughtful. His menu reflects that he cares about my eating preferences. That's really sweet."

"So, you're not bothered at all that he takes photos of us without permission or how he knows you're a vegetarian?"

She thought about it. "I guess I could be if I wanted to be. I don't live in some perfect fantasy in my head. Awful things happen every day and I wish they didn't. I try to balance the world by being the best person I can be. I know that's not enough, but it's what I'm able to do. I understand Clay might be doing this more for himself than us, but that doesn't stop me from loving that he is trying to bring us together." She smoothed her napkin over her lap. "I should warn you that I made him promise to find someone for you if we don't work out."

"Why would you do that?"

He needed the truth as much as she needed to say it. "Because I like to see you smile. And despite what you think, you deserve to be happy."

If it was possible for a hulking, intimidating man to look uncertain and huggable, that was how Bradford appeared to Joanna. If they'd been alone or in a more stable place with each other she would have gotten up and given him a long, tight hug.

He frowned. "Don't—"

"Swear? Jinx. You owe me a dollar," she cut him off with a joke to lighten the mood.

He cocked his head slightly to one side. "What is it with you and small amounts of money?"

"What would you rather owe me?" Her question hung in the air between them, completely changing the focus of their conversation.

His grin was pure devilish charm. "If you're ever lucky enough to be with me, I'll tell you."

She'd never found a man sexier. His eyes were unguarded and the world fell away as she gazed into them. "You're quite the ballbuster, I see."

"I'm confident you can give as good as you get."

Before she had a chance to respond, the server was back asking if they were ready to order. Joanna ordered a water, a bowl of fruit, a side of granola, and yogurt.

Bradford said, "Just coffee. Black."

She looked the menu over again. "He'll have the Oreo pancakes."

He didn't correct her but after the server left the table, he gave her a long look.

She raised her shoulders as well as both hands and shamelessly said, "I'm trying to eat healthy, but they sound delicious."

"Did you order them for me or for you?"

She made a show of looking innocent. "I know you don't eat breakfast but this was an opportunity I felt you shouldn't miss." She couldn't hold her smile back. "Also, one bite off your plate won't kill my diet."

He threw back his head and laughed. They sat there simply smiling at each other like two teenagers on a first date. Their drinks were delivered as well as their food. Alone again, Bradford asked, "What if I'm not the type to share?"

"You'd make an exception for me." She rested her chin on her hand and fluttered her eyelashes at him. "Because you like me."

He leaned across the space between them, cupped her chin, and brought her face to his. He claimed her mouth with confidence. His was not a kiss from a boy—but from an experienced man who knew what he wanted.

Her lips quivered under his then opened when his tongue darted across them. He wasn't gentle, nor did he rush. In that kiss she found a hint of what sex between them might be like and it brought being with him to a whole new level. She'd had sex, even good sex, but nothing she'd ever had trouble walking away from. Bradford was building a hunger in her, a slow burn of need that was so intense it scared her a little.

She broke off the kiss and sat back.

He settled into his seat as well.

They were both breathing raggedly.

After their breakfast was served, he cut into his mountain of pancakes, stabbed his fork through a decadent pile, and held it up for her to take. "The only thing I can't imagine sharing is you."

She let him feed her in a way she'd always thought was corny when she'd seen other couples do it. It didn't feel corny at all. It felt wildly intimate to be fed by him. She chewed, swallowed, then said, "In that regard, I'm not good at sharing either."

"Tell me something about yourself."

She filled a spoon with berries. "What would you like to know?"

"Anything. Everything."

Although she would have rather heard about his life, she started to tell him about hers because he seemed to be seeking something. "I was raised on a small farm. Nothing fancy. We had horses, chickens, and whatever animal people asked us to help them rehome. I don't remember a time when my day didn't start with barn chores. Dad worked as an IT tech for a local bank. Mom still owns a florist shop. They're both mostly retired now, but they still take in animals others might call throwaways."

"Sounds crowded."

"Not really. Rescues aren't when their goal is to rehabili-
tate and rehome. A few stay, either because my parents fall in
love with them or because they're too broken for anyone else
to want."

His face tightened. "Is that what this is? You think you
can *rescue* me?"

She could have lied, but he wouldn't have believed her.
"I'll admit that when I first met you I just wanted to hug
you." He looked uncomfortable with her admission, so she
added, "Now I'm open to that and where that hug might
take us."

Desire flamed in his eyes. "You are surprisingly direct."

"Not usually."

The air was charged with sexual tension again. He
cleared his throat. "You moved closer to the city for college.
I'm surprised you didn't move back."

She took a bite of her fruit before answering. "I live close
enough to visit my parents once a week, but far enough to
have my own life. I have amazing parents, but if my mother
could, she would still be making my bed and reading my
diary."

"You keep a diary?"

"I kept one for her." Joanna smiled as she reminisced. "I
was in my early teens when I suspected she was reading the
real one I had. Spitefully, I wrote a few wild entries that had
her flipping out with worry. I was so angry with her I didn't
care. When my father found out what I'd done, he suggested
I write everything I felt in my diary and leave it out for her to

read. I did. And she answered me on the next page."

"And said you were grounded?"

"No, she apologized and explained how losing her father had left her with a fear of losing everyone she loved. We wrote back and forth to each other in journals straight through college."

"That's—" He didn't seem to have a word for it.

She supplied, "beautiful."

"Yes."

"Were your parents—?"

"No."

She almost said she was sorry, but they'd been down that road before and he didn't want her sympathy. Instead, she said, "Anyway, while at college I met Aly and Angelina. We hit it off and they've also become family to me."

He let out a long breath. "I don't have a family nor am I looking for one."

She could have let him have that claim, but that wasn't what she'd witnessed. "That's not true. You and Ian have a bond that some might argue is stronger than a blood tie."

"Ian's the exception."

"Connor absolutely adores you. And before you say anything I won't believe—just admit you like him too."

"He's a good guy and he's hilarious."

"Family comes in all shapes and sizes. The mistake people make is thinking it has to be one certain way to be good. That's just not true."

His eyes narrowed. "Before you say anything I won't believe—your definition of family includes marriage, kids, trips to Disney?"

She wagged a finger at him. "It does and no one can make me feel bad about it. I want to raise a whole herd of children and teach them all how to muck stalls and chase chickens. My dreams don't require anyone's validation. I know what I want."

He shook his head and opened his mouth to say something then snapped it shut. They ate without speaking for a few minutes.

The server returned to clear their plates. As soon as he left, the man who had initially greeted them returned. "Are you ready?"

"For?" Bradford asked, rising to his feet.

Joanna grabbed her purse and stood as well. Bradford held out his hand and she took it without hesitation. Her heart was racing with a combination of his nearness and anticipation of what else Clay might have prepared for them.

The man pointed to an opening that led deeper into the tent. "For the ball. Follow me, please."

Bradford leaned down and said, "If I admit I'm curious about what's next that doesn't mean I agree with Clay's heavy-handedness."

Joanna smiled up at him. "Of course not." She gave into an impulse and hugged his side. "I'm excited too."

Chapter Seven

B RADFORD WASN'T NORMALLY surprised by much, but as he stepped into the next part of the tent he had to admit that someone, likely not Clay himself, had done an impressive job of creating a cohesive theme.

The section was significantly larger than the one they'd left, fifty by a hundred feet was his guess. All white background from the flooring to the solid walls right up to the solid but twinkling white ceiling. He immediately noted two exits: the one they'd just entered and one at the far end of the room.

Scattered around the room were ball games like one might find in an arcade—all clear with white and black accents. Impressive in their uniqueness. The basketball throw had a clear acrylic base with black accents on the hoop. The balls in the basket beside it were similar, transparent except for their black lines.

Farther on was a clear bowling alley that looked like an ice sculpture but seemed to be made of acrylic as well. Next to it was a line of what looked like crystal balls. All of it was accented in white. There was a black-and-white pinball machine beside a similar skeet ball target area with small clear balls the size of grapefruits.

On the wall in gold lettering a sign read: Welcome to the Ball Room.

Clever.

Are you okay, Clay? We need to talk about how seriously you're taking this fairy godfather shit.

"This is amazing!" Joanna said, hugging him with an enthusiasm she couldn't contain. The room and everything else ceased to matter. There was only her and the heat searing through him every place her body moved over his.

Amazing? He'd say it was fucking scary how easy it was for her to overwhelm his senses. "It's something alright."

She leaned back and smiled up at him. "Are you afraid of a little competition? Big man worried I might kick his ass at a ball throw?"

He looped his arms around her hips and settled her against his growing excitement. "That's not where my mind currently is at all."

Her mouth rounded and he gave in to the need to taste her again. Her arms came up and around his neck. He bent his head and kissed her with all the hunger dammed up within him. It was a greedy claiming, a concession to something he'd tried to deny. She met his kiss with equal passion. Her mouth opened to his, their tongues swirled and withdrew. She moaned with pleasure and he shuddered.

Had they been alone, clothing would have started flying, but a small voice in his head warned him to keep a foot in reality. He raised his head and rested his forehead on hers.

"Let's get out of here."

Her breath tickled his lips. She hesitated, but then in a near whisper said, "Okay."

He stepped back, took her hand in his, and turned to lead her out of the room only to see the way they'd entered was closed without a handle. Like a door to a hidden room, it blended with the rest of the wall. Bradford whipped around. The far exit had also been closed and disguised. "Fucking Clay."

As long as it was Clay.

The setup was too extravagant for a normal hit. There were definitely less expensive ways to take him out if someone wanted Bradford dead.

What angered him was how easily he'd lowered his guard. His hand tightened on Joanna's. One fucking date that wasn't even really a date and he'd already put her life in danger.

"You okay?" Joanna asked.

"Not really," he snapped. He didn't want to alarm her so he lied. "I'm uncomfortable in small places."

She looked around. The room they were locked in was huge, but that didn't stop her from looking sympathetic when her eyes met his again. "I can understand that. Let's see if we can find someone who'll let us out."

On a table beside the door where they'd come in was a tablet and a white card with instructions. "Tap the screen. Play the video."

First Bradford checked for wires or any sign that it might be rigged to explode. When he found none, he tapped the screen and hit play on the video that came up.

Clay's face filled the screen. "Hi, Joanna. Isn't this place incredible? You're welcome. Bradford, I'm proud of you for getting this far, and I apologize ahead of time for locking you in. Trust is such an important part of any relationship but so is having fun together. Think of this as an escape room where you have to learn to play together for the doors to reopen."

Bradford growled, "I'm not fucking—"

Clay's video continued, "Before you threaten to break out on your own, being in a healthy relationship means taking your partner's feelings into consideration. Lexi's happiness is as important as my own. We all know you're perfectly capable of breaking out if you want to, but before you do that, ask Joanna if that's what she wants."

He looked down at Joanna's face. She seemed conflicted. He remembered what she'd said earlier about wondering if their differences were too much for them to overcome. She'd wished he could see all this through her eyes.

He took a deep breath and pushed aside how angry he was for not noticing when the man in the tux had left the room. Joanna likely didn't see any of this in that light. The truth was there in her eyes, she was enjoying Clay's antics.

Staying gave Clay control of the situation and Bradford wasn't comfortable with that, but as he watched the hope in Joanna's eyes dim, he was forced to acknowledge an uncomfortable truth: *I care about this woman. Her happiness does matter to me.*

"You want to stay and play," he said.

Her chin rose slightly, but the smile had gone from her eyes. "Yes."

In or out. She wasn't someone he wanted to fuck once and forget. It was time to step up or step off. "I do too."

Her expression was cautiously excited. "Really? I know it's over the top. You don't have to do this for me."

He thought about how close they'd come to leaving and heading to either his place or hers. She would have gone with him because she trusted him, but what had he done to earn that trust? How had he valued it?

I'm not looking for a relationship—healthy or otherwise.
Then what am I doing?
I'm staying.
Not because both doors are locked, but because . . . "I want to."

She bounced beside him. "I promise I'll go easy on you."

"Oh, really?" He pulled her close, bending her slightly back over his arm. "What makes you think you'll have to?"

She brought a hand up to caress his cheek. As a rule, he told people not to touch his face, especially not his scars, but her touch was welcome anywhere. The smile she gave him was cheeky. "Because I'm so cute it'll be impossible for you to concentrate."

"You've got me there."

He kissed her again and reveled in the sweetness of it. He'd been with some women with nearly professional skills, but none had come close to affecting him the way Joanna did. She didn't hold back when she kissed. She was openly enthusiastic as well as playful. When the heat rose between them to the point where he was ready to once again suggest they leave, she gave him one last kiss and laughed. "Now, which game would you like to lose at first?"

He chuckled. "You choose."

She took his hand and looked around. "I've done escape rooms at the mall, but I have no idea where to start here. The only thing he said was we'd have to learn to play together for the doors to open."

Clay's no Einstein; I'm sure we'll figure it out. He scanned the room. There were small cameras above each game. On closer inspection the floor wasn't solid. The strips in it could be sensors. Was Clay watching? Bradford looked right into a camera and let his expression convey his warning. *The harder you make this on me, the harder I'll make it on you when I get out.*

"Look, the basketball throw is blinking," Joanna exclaimed.

Bradford tipped his head at the camera. *Smart man.* "Let's start there, then."

They walked over to the game together but separated when they reached it. Joanna picked up one of the clear basketballs, tossed it straight in the air, then caught it. "You have to admit this is cool." Bradford chose one for himself.

She took a practice shot.

It went straight in but no points came up on the board. Bradford threw his with the same result.

"I don't understand," she said. "How do we play this game together?"

Bradford shook his head. "You're asking the wrong person."

Joanna chose another ball. "Let's play around the world."

"What?"

Her eyebrows rose. "You've never played around the world?"

"I was never into sports."

"It's a two-person game. All you need is one friend."

He said nothing, because the truth wasn't something that belonged in the game tent. Outside of Ian and Connor, he'd never really had a friend. Friendship required trust and trust was something he struggled with.

She cocked her head to one side, then said, "Right. Okay, well it's an easy enough game and you already know how to shoot. We'll keep it simple. I'll try to make the shot while you try to stop me. If I miss, you take the next shot while I try to block you. I make the shot, I get to shoot again. We stop when one of us gets to . . . let's say five to keep it short. Usually people go to twenty-one."

She moved a distance from the game.

He turned and stood in front of it.

She began to dribble the ball, moving back and forth. He stood his ground. There was no way she could get around him where he was.

She paused and held the ball under one of her arms. "Aren't you going to move?"

"Don't have to. You don't have a clear shot."

She sighed. "That's true, but your way is no fun. You're supposed to try to take the ball from me."

"To do so I'd have to leave the net wide open."

She began to dribble again. "Exactly."

He moved toward her, she darted around him and made the shot. Her joyful laugh took all the sting out of her win. A point went up on the board.

"That's one for me." She retrieved the ball and returned to her original spot. "You'll have to try harder."

He was better prepared the second time. When he stepped forward and she tried to skirt around him, he threw out an arm and easily scooped her up. Momentum brought her against his chest with a thud. Slowly, oh so slowly, she slid down the front of him.

Her cheeks were flushed and her eyes were dark with desire. He was painfully excited. Her laugh bounced her breasts against his chest, scrambling his thoughts. "That's technically cheating," she said in a husky voice. "Not complaining, just stating it's against the usual rules."

He took the ball from her and threw it toward the hoop without taking his eyes from hers. It binged with another point. He'd said he'd never played with anyone else, but that didn't mean he hadn't practiced tossing balls to pass the time at his foster family's home. "Whose rules? We don't need them."

"Right," she answered, looking a lot more eager to kiss him than take another shot. "Still, basketball is not a hands-on sport."

"Then why the hell are we playing it?" he joked. Having her pressed up against him felt too good for him to care about anything else.

She laughed again. "I love this side of you."

He tensed as the word love ricocheted through him but then laughed at himself for reading so much into her innocent statement. After giving her a quick kiss, he set her back from him and said, "Let's do this."

He tried to block her next shot with moves he'd seen in movies. She made it past him and got the point. He stole the ball from her the next time and made the next point.

When he stood there dribbling the ball while she danced around him he couldn't have cared less about who won the game. Her eyes were focused on his hands, she was flushed with excitement, and he'd never seen anything more beautiful. He could have watched her all day.

She took the ball away from him and made the shot, then turned back, hand on hip and said, "You let me have that one."

He grinned at her. "I did."

She grabbed the ball then sashayed by him. "Winner decides where we go on our next date."

"Hey." He positioned himself in front of her, readying to steal the ball from her again. "You can't change the rules now."

"Rules? Whose? Ours, I think. And I see an easy win in my future."

Oh, really? He braced his hands on his knees. "Bring it."

She made the shot and missed. He retrieved the ball and sank it.

She couldn't stop his next shot or the one after that.

He deliberately missed so she could have the ball back. As they played together it became easier to anticipate her moves. When she went left, he went with her. When she went right he did as well. It was a dance of sorts that had him smiling more than he could ever remember doing.

She wasn't getting past him and she knew it. She pointed to somewhere behind him. "Look the door's open."

He glanced away, confirmed it wasn't true, and lifted her off her feet again as she tried to make it past him. This time, though, she anticipated his move as well and threw the ball just before she hit his chest. The winning point rang out as did her laughter.

He lifted her above him. "You're a little cheat," he teased.

"It's called diversion. Not my fault you fell for it." Her hands went to his shoulders.

"Where's the referee?"

Her eyes were sparkling with laughter. "Why, do you want a redo?"

He slid her down the front of him. "No, I want to know if there's a penalty for this." He claimed her mouth and brought her full against his hard cock. She clutched at his back. He dug his hands into her hair. They kissed until he felt like a young man afraid to explode in his pants. *Holy shit.*

She was breathing as heavily as he was. They stood in each other's arms for several minutes as he told himself to calm the fuck down.

"The bowling alley lit up," she said just above a whisper.

He didn't want to like anything about the tent, but she was glowing and her happiness filled him with a lightness he wasn't ready to label. All he knew was it felt good, damn good, to be laughing with her. "Have you ever bowled?" he asked.

"Once or twice as a kid. Nothing recent."

"Then we'll figure it out together."

"I'd like that." She settled herself under his arm as they walked, and nothing had ever felt so right.

AS THEY WALKED to the bowling alley, Joanna reflected on how different Bradford was from any man she'd been with. He didn't play by the rules. *"Whose rules?"* His voice echoed in her mind. She snuck a look up at him.

There was no longer any doubt about whether or not he was attracted to her, but their connection felt deeper than that. He was letting her in, showing her sides of him he normally protected and that made every smile he gave her special.

He caught her looking at him and frowned. "What?"

She hugged his side tighter. "Nothing. Just happy we stayed."

"That's because you haven't seen me bowl yet."

"I'm serious. This was good for us."

He tensed. "Joanna—"

She gave him a light pinch on those rock-hard abs of his. "Don't even say there is no us. I'm here. You're here. We are a pronoun. I understand this could lead to the two of us having great sex and still not knowing if it can go anywhere. Sometimes you just have to breathe, not worry about everything that can go wrong, and enjoy the moment."

He stopped and turned her in his arms. "It's important

to me that whatever happens between us—you don't get hurt."

"That's what's most important to me as well, but about you. I'm not a child, Bradford. Technically, every relationship I had before you fizzled out. Was it me? Them? Both? I don't know. All I can do is be me and keep going forward with faith that eventually I'll find the right person. I refuse to believe I'm meant to be alone." She tapped his chest lightly. "I refuse to believe you are either."

He didn't say anything, but Joanna took that as a good sign. Bradford kept most of his thoughts to himself. Somewhere along the way he must have learned that was safer. There were times when he reminded her of a new rescue who wanted to trust the humans attempting to help them but couldn't get past memories of abuse. Clarity, consistency, and kindness were the keys to winning animals over and she hoped that same recipe would work with Bradford.

Did she want to have sex with him? *Hell, yes.*

She wouldn't though, if she thought it would only confuse him more. "I have an idea."

He waited without speaking.

She continued, "If I win at bowling, we don't worry about where this is going and just enjoy hanging out together."

"And if you lose?"

"I accuse you of cheating, and then we still don't worry about anything beyond if we enjoy hanging out."

His frown deepened. "That's not fair to you."

She put a hand on her hip. "Last time I checked I didn't

actually need a man. Sure, I like the idea of one in my life and it's easier to have a family with one around, but I'm doing pretty damn well on my own. You worry about you and I'll worry about me."

He nodded and then walked over to where the candlepin balls were. He paused before picking one up. "You weren't the bad fuck."

She remembered he'd said that she might be—based on her relationship history. It might have made her defensive had he said it in another place or time, but she was too happy. "Funny, but we have to work on your complimenting skills." She also picked up a ball.

"It wasn't meant as a compliment, just an observation." His tone was serious but there was humor in his eyes.

She decided a change of topic was in order. "So, I get the idea of this game. I believe we get three tries instead of two. There's a strike and a spare, but I don't really know how to keep score."

Bradford studied the alley and the immediate area around it. "I don't see a scoreboard."

"Do you think that's the point? Couples shouldn't keep score against each other?"

"Could be." He looked at one of the cameras. "Although I can't say Clay is who I'd look to for advice on how to make a relationship work."

Without filtering herself, Joanna blurted, "That's so much better than what I thought you were going to say." His head snapped around so he was facing her. She raised her shoulders and shot him an apologetic smile. "I just heard you in my head countering with—*We're not a couple.*" She deepened her voice for the last part for effect.

The corner of his mouth twitched. "Is that how I sound?"

She cleared her throat and in an even deeper tone said, *"I don't do relationships."*

"I see." His expression didn't change and for a moment she worried that she'd offended him. His next words, however, were in a high-pitched attempt of her voice. *"I want a relationship, but it doesn't have to be with you . . . any Prince Charming who doesn't swear and believes in unicorns and magic will be a great father for my future ten kids."*

She held the crystal ball out in front of her and mimicked his voice again, *"Unicorns? I eat them for breakfast—along with anyone who crosses me."*

He laughed.

She did as well.

He stepped closer and ran a hand through her hair. "I love that you're not afraid of me."

She went onto her tiptoes and whispered in his ear, "I love that you *are.*" Before things got too heated, she retreated and sent her ball down the crystal alley toward the frosted pins with black trim. Her ball veered right and rolled most of the way in the gutter.

He handed her the ball he was holding then positioned himself right behind her. In a fuck-me now voice he said, "I'm no expert, but the problem was in your arm." Then he ran a hand down her arm, sending all kinds of heat rushing through her. "Try to keep it straight when you toss the ball."

She closed her eyes briefly, loving the feel of him all around her. It made her wish they'd chosen to leave while also feeling grateful they'd stayed. Sex with him probably would be good either way, but she was easily imagining the two of them naked and tangled on her bed—or her floor— or his bed—or his floor.

"And focus," he growled.

"You're making it a little hard."

"So are you." His chuckle was so sexy she nearly turned and launched herself at him. She didn't though, because the anticipation was excruciatingly wonderful.

She shifted her body so her ass brushed against his thighs and his bulging cock. "I had no idea bowling was such an exciting sport."

"Throw the damn ball. The sooner we get through these games—"

She took slow aim and brought her arm back. He stayed right behind her, his breath a warm tickle on her neck. When she released the ball, he kissed his way up her neck to the tip of her ear. "Better."

He was, but her throw? She had no idea nor did she care. Her body was humming for him in a way that made everything beyond him fade away.

The sound of the ball cracking into pins barely caught her attention. She turned and searched Bradford's face. "It's not usually like this for me."

His hands found her hips. "Bowling?"

She ran a hand over his cheek then tapped his chin with a finger. "You know what I'm talking about."

He visibly took a breath. "I do."

"And?"

She could almost see him withdraw mentally. "What do you want me to say?"

"Nothing you don't mean."

"A moment ago, you told me neither of us should worry about where this is going."

She had. And she'd meant it. "I'm not talking about to-morrow; I'm talking about right here and now. I've never felt this way with someone before. I'm looking for some hint that this isn't normal for you."

With his gaze still shuttered, he said, "I can honestly say nothing about this is normal."

She shook her head and looked away. She'd been hoping for more, but she didn't want to push him. He'd been honest about his history and his issues. Just how magical did she think the tent was? *Hello, reality. My name is Joanna. Sometimes I lose sight of you.*

He pulled her closer. The look on his face was harsh, but his tone wasn't. "I'm not good with words, but I'd take a bullet for you."

She placed a hand flat on his chest. "I'm reasonably certain you'd take a bullet for almost anyone you saw in danger."

"True."

He needed smaller steps, less pressure. "But would you muck a stall for anyone?"

"Excuse me?"

"I have a farm to get back to and those stalls don't clean

themselves. I'll be up early tomorrow morning cleaning my barn—would you like to help me?" When he didn't immediately answer, she added, "I did win the ball toss which allows me to choose our next date."

His head tipped back as he considered her offer. "And that's what you want?"

She shrugged. "I'm not fancy, and I'd love to show you my little farm."

"Okay." The kiss that followed was all honey and promise. When he raised his head, he said, "But then I choose our next date."

Next date.

For someone who doesn't do the see-you-tomorrow thing, he said that pretty easily.

"You're on."

Something behind her caught his attention and he said, "The alley light just went out but the pinball machine lit up. Looks like we're moving on."

It sure does.

"I should warn you," she said as she took him by the hand and began to lead him toward the pinball machine, "we had a pinball machine in our garage. I don't want to brag, but this is my game."

He leaned down so his lips caressed her ear as he murmured, "Then this time you take the lead."

She met his gaze and was reminded of something her father often said: "A strong man is gentle because he doesn't need to prove his strength and a weak man is cruel because he does." Bradford had definitely learned to protect himself and he'd lost faith that he deserved happiness, but she was looking forward to seeing him with her mini-horses. If he was half the man her gut told her he was, they would adore him.

His expression closed again. "Don't look at me like that."

"Like what?"

"Like I'm someone I'm not."

The sadness was back in his eyes and her heart ached for him. Her hands went to his face. She ran her fingertips lightly over his scar. "I do what I want."

He caught her hand and kissed it before lowering it. "What am I going to do with you?"

She grinned up at him. "Now or when we get back to my place?"

He sucked in a breath. "You're dangerous."

She smiled at him and stepped back. "Don't you forget it. Now get your ass over to that pinball machine and show me what you've got."

Chapter Eight

B Y THE TIME the final game light went off and the doors swung open, Bradford wasn't sure he wanted to step back into reality. He couldn't remember the last time he'd let go and had fun, but that's what the past couple of hours had been. He retrieved Joanna's purse for her, and with a hand on her lower back, guided her out of the tent. On the way out, they passed a chiming clock that announced twelve noon as if it were midnight.

Oh, Clay.

The sun was still high in the sky. The sounds of a family walking by on the path broke the silence. Everything felt a bit surreal.

He was tempted to suggest they go directly to her place, but if he intended to stay and help her clean in the morning, a change of clothing might be nice. He didn't want to separate from her, but he also refused to be someone who couldn't. "If you want company tonight I should collect a few things from my place."

She blushed but held his gaze. "I would love company. I'm also a really good cook. What's your favorite food?"

"I don't know that I have one." Food had been scarce early in his life and he'd learned to eat to survive rather than care what it tasted like.

"No meat. Is that okay?"

"As long as you don't try to make a soybean look like a steak, I'm fine with whatever."

She smiled and almost took his hand then hesitated and didn't. He understood. Outside of the tent they were back in reality and although it didn't change how much he wanted her, it did apply the brakes a bit on what had been a runaway train. As they made their way down the path she said, "Do you need my address?"

He answered with just a look.

She continued, "Right, you know everything about me already."

They walked in silence for a few minutes. He struggled to maintain his usual cool. He'd never been the type to hold a woman's hand in public, but the absence of her touch was like a dull ache. She wasn't bouncing with joy. Her cheeks were no longer flushed with passion. *I'm doing this. I'm killing the vibe.*

He had no idea what men said to keep a romantic mood going since that had never been his goal. He'd always kept things straightforward so there were no hurt feelings when he didn't call the next day.

This was different.

He opened his mouth to say something, decided against it, and almost said something else before deciding against that as well. The sound of frustration he emitted brought a side glance from Joanna, but she didn't address it.

I'm just going to say it. "I want to do this better than I am."

She stopped. "What?"

He swallowed hard. "Us."

Her eyes shone with emotion, and she gave him a full-body hug. Against his chest, she murmured, "You're doing fine."

He kissed the top of her head. "I've always been a lot better at leaving than I've been at staying."

"So have I." She tipped her head back and looked up at him. "I don't want to break your heart."

"I don't want to get you killed."

She tensed against him. "I don't want you to get me killed either. Is that an imminent possibility?"

He sighed. "No one does what I've done without making enemies."

"I could say the same."

"The children's book industry is cutthroat?" He hadn't meant to sound as sarcastic as he had, but she wasn't taking his concern seriously.

She stepped out of his embrace. "I was referring to some of the people I've had run-ins with via horse kill lots. For everyone who thinks what I do is wonderful there is someone with an opposing view. I received death threats last year after I brought attention to a seller who was forging paperwork for horses. It got ugly for a little while."

"Why did no one I spoke to mention that?"

"Because I didn't tell anyone. I didn't want them to worry."

"Did you go to the police?"

"No. I ignored the messages until they stopped. I don't engage with crazy."

When, not if, he found out who had been threatening her, they would think twice before hassling any woman. "You live alone. And I know you don't own a gun."

"There's usually someone around. I have volunteers and trainers who work with the horses. I refuse to live my life in fear."

"So you ignored the threats?"

"Yes."

Oh, my God. "If anyone ever threatens you again, tell me."

"And you'll handle it?"

"Absolutely."

"I'm not sure I'd want you to. Nothing happened. The guy was just talking shit."

His stomach was churning and his hands clenched at his sides. "You were lucky."

She gave him a look. "Nothing happened, Bradford. Seriously, and it's been over a year."

Neither said anything for several long minutes. Finally, she said, "I'm sorry, I didn't say that to upset you. I just wanted to show you that a person doesn't have to be an international spy or whatever you are to have enemies."

"It's fine. And how you handled that situation is actually none of my business." He still felt a little sick from imagining anyone hurting her. Being with her was bringing to the surface emotions he usually kept in check. They'd just started spending time together and he was already a wreck on the inside. It was too late though to simply walk away. The damage was already done. She'd given him an Achilles' heel.

They didn't speak again until they were at her car. He felt like a complete ass for ruining what had been an amazing day. He stood over her beside her car and looked down into her eyes while trying to figure out what the fuck to say.

She laid a hand on his chest and he wondered if she could feel the heavy thud of his heart. "Bradford?"

"Yes?"

"We had a good day." She smiled. "A really good day. You don't have to come over tonight if you're not ready to."

"If I'm not *ready*?" He closed his eyes briefly. *What the fuck is she talking about?* His mood took more of a dive as a possible translation came to him. His tone turned defensive. "Tell me if you've changed your mind."

Her eyebrows rose. "Is that what you want?"

He frowned. "Don't dance around the truth. You either have or you haven't."

"Breathe." She stepped closer, placing her other hand on his chest as well.

He almost told her he didn't require coaching on how to hold his shit together, but she was giving that sweet look again—the one he found impossible to resist. He took one deep breath then another. His stomach calmed and the adrenaline that had begun to pump through him subsided.

"Better?" she asked.

The answer to that question completely depends on if she's referring to the acid in my stomach or the clarity of my thought process. I'm no longer in need of an antacid, but I also have no fucking idea what I should do next.

Stay and protect her, even if being with me might put her in danger?

Buy fucking flowers and show up at her door tonight like some domesticated clown?

Have sex with her because it's what we both want?

Wait because she deserves better than I've given women in the past?

His stomach started to churn again.

She slid her hands up his chest and around his neck, urging his head to lower. When his face was just above hers she gave him a tender kiss unlike any he'd experienced before. It shook him to the core. He pulled her closer.

Passion flared between them, but it didn't muddle the message she was sending. Everything he needed from her was in that kiss—confidence, desire, patience. He had no idea if she could read him as easily, but he was coming to a decision. He wanted this in his life—her in his life.

He set her back from him. "How does six sound? I need time to—" He lied on a regular basis; it was how he gained access or covered his tracks. He couldn't lie to her, though. Not when she was looking up at him with more trust than he'd earned.

Her smile was easy and open. "Perfect. That will give me plenty of time to get a few things, spend some time at the barn, and fit in a shower if I'm lucky."

He groaned. Now all he could think about was her in the

shower. He needed to put some distance between the two of them so he could unscramble his thoughts. "Do you want me to bring anything?"

She opened her car door. "I have a pool. Bring swim trunks." She winked. "Or not. I'm open to swimming either way." With that she closed the door of her car, started her engine, and pulled out.

He thought she'd drive away, but she waited. She was sticking around to make sure his car started before pulling away. He'd done that countless times for others, but no one had ever done it for him. He climbed into his own car and revved its engine. She waved at him. He waved back. She was smiling. He looked at himself in his rearview mirror. Damned if he wasn't grinning from ear to ear.

On his drive back to his place, his phone rang. He was more of a texter than a talker, but it was Sophie Barrington so he answered. He'd made the mistake of giving her his phone number when she'd asked for it in Oklahoma. He thought she'd use it for emergencies, but instead she'd started calling him once a week to "check in." No one he knew did that.

Worse, if he didn't answer, she not only called back, but so did Ian—telling him to stop worrying his mother and answer his damn phone. As far as he could tell there was no delicate way to extricate himself from the situation, so for the present he was dealing with it.

"Hi, Sophie."

"Bradford, I hope this isn't a bad time."

Was there a good time for the awkward conversations

they engaged in? "Good as any."

"I was sorry to see you leave early last night. I spoke to Clay about his behavior. He said he'd give you some space."

"Did he?" He fought to keep sarcasm out of his voice. "I appreciate your concern, Sophie, but he wasn't why I left. I had somewhere I needed to be."

"Of course. Dale told me I was likely worried about nothing, but that's who I am. I can't turn it off. So, you and Joanna seemed to be getting along."

He didn't respond to that, but if Sophie were anyone else he would have told her to mind her own business.

She continued, "Connor told me a group of them are heading over to Iceland soon to watch Dylan film. He said you were invited but declined."

"My schedule doesn't allow for it."

"I realize I might be overstepping, but I care about you. You should go, Bradford. Those boys love you. Not only would it mean a lot to them to have you there, but it would be good for you."

"Sophie—"

"I hear Joanna is going. What a great way for you to get to know her better. See if anything develops."

"Sophie—"

"She's such a good soul. Her mini-rescue—so inspirational. And her family? Pure gold. Nicest people. She's also smart as a whip. Not a pushover at all. You'd do well with someone like that."

"I—"

"Women like that don't stay single long. Initially she

seemed interested in Dylan, but I'm glad that foolishness is over. I couldn't picture the two of them together. But you? I hope you reconsider the Iceland trip. It might surprise you how much the two of you have in common."

"Sophie—"

"Just promise to consider it."

He sighed. "I will."

"Dale and I are in the New York area for a few more days. We're having a nice quiet dinner tonight. We'd love company."

If there was one thing the matriarch of the Barrington family never was, it was alone. He wasn't falling for it. "Regretfully, I already have plans."

"Oh, anything special?"

"Nothing I'm comfortable discussing yet." He should have said a simple no, but seeing Joanna again felt too important to dismiss even if doing so would have made his life easier.

Sophie called out to her husband. "Dale, I think Bradford met someone. He said he has plans he's not comfortable discussing yet."

Dale came onto the call via another line. "Bradford."

"Sir." There really was no other way to greet a man like Dale. He personified quiet dignity.

Dale continued, "I can see how a date would trump dinner with us, but I do hope you bring her around. Anyone who is important to you is important to us."

In an excited tone, Sophie asked, "If I call Joanna will she also say she's busy tonight?"

Dale cut in, "Sophie, let the boy be. They're both adults. If something develops between them, they'll tell us when they're ready to."

"She would be so good for him," Sophie defended. "If it is her, Bradford, take a gift for her ponies. That would make the biggest impact."

"And be yourself," Dale added. "Joanna comes across as the type who cares more about a man's integrity than the car he drives. She does quite well with those books of hers, but she's humble about it. Very down-to-earth. We adore her."

Bradford wanted to deny he was seeing Joanna. The lie was on the tip of his tongue, but he didn't utter it. Instead he maintained his silence.

"Her mother told me her favorite dessert is strawberry shortcake," Sophie said.

"Sophie," Dale admonished, "did you pump Joanna's family for information about her?"

"Hardly. Lydia would like to see her happily married as much as I would. When I told her we had several eligible bachelors in the family, she freely told me more than I ever would have inquired about."

"Sophie," Dale said, "didn't you just tell Clay to stay out of Bradford's private life?"

"How can sharing with Bradford what Joanna likes for dessert be an intrusion?"

Bradford parked his car and cut the engine. "I just pulled into my garage. I'll probably lose this call when my phone disconnects from Bluetooth so I'll say goodbye now."

Dale answered first. "Come by to see us soon, son. Come

alone or bring someone, doesn't matter. You're always welcome."

Bradford was never quite comfortable with the Barringtons' display of affection for him so he mumbled a thank you. Even as he was ending the call, he heard Sophie say, "Something for the ponies and strawberry shortcake for her. Good luck, Bradford."

He got out of his car, pocketed his phone, then took Joanna's gift from the back seat. His thoughts were in a tailspin. Outside of the missions he'd gone on with Ian, Bradford had lived the life of a loner. He rented several apartments all over the world, but owned virtually nothing. Life was easier when he had nothing to hold him anywhere.

Joanna was firmly planted in New Jersey. He lived a global life. How much would his lifestyle have to change to be with her? More importantly, how much was he willing to change?

He let himself into his apartment then stood in the middle of the living room. He'd rented it furnished, changed nothing about it, and had no attachment to anything in it. *Is this how I always want to live?*

Joanna's question came back to him: *"What's your favorite food?"*

He wanted to have one.

What did it mean that he didn't?

His apartment represented how he lived his life—no attachments. Ian was the closest to a friend Bradford had. Historically, they'd only called each other when they needed help. They saved each other's asses but didn't go further into each other's lives. Lately Ian and his family had begun to invite Bradford to social events and family gatherings.

I haven't let myself get attached to him or his family.

I made sure I had nothing to lose.

Nothing worth living for.

Is that how things have to be or am I the coward Clay accused me of being?

He put the swear jar on the table. It was the only personal item in the room. He spent a long moment simply staring at it while his conversation with Sophie and Dale echoed in his mind. They hovered over him, attentive in a way no one had ever been with him—until Joanna.

His lifestyle didn't allow for attachments.

Ian makes it work somehow.

Bradford headed into his bedroom, took out an overnight bag, put it on his bed, but didn't immediately start to fill it. Instead he sat beside it and bent forward, bracing his elbows on his knees. It wasn't too late to end things with Joanna. Her feelings would be hurt, but neither had invested much into the other yet.

Sex wasn't something he normally put so much thought into. If the woman was interested and he was attracted— good enough. *Why am I making this such a big deal?*

Because it is.

I care about her.

Really care.

He laughed at himself. *It's not just about putting her in danger.*

Not if I'm honest.

The idea of having feelings for anyone scares the shit out of me.

He thought about Joanna's grandfather and how she saw his suicide as a win for the men he'd killed. His own death would be celebrated by many people who were still alive as well as those he'd sent over to the other side.

He didn't like how easily he understood what would drive a man to end his own life. Joanna's grandfather sounded like he'd been a good man. *A better man than I am.* He'd committed to one woman, raised a family, probably worked a fucking job he hated because his family's happiness mattered more to him than his own.

But he still took his life.

Why?

Is that the future I'd bring Joanna and any children we'd have?

Are some people too far gone?

He took a deep breath and spoke to something larger than himself, if something like that existed. "I'm not afraid of death. If there's anything after this life I know I'm headed nowhere good. I don't expect absolution for what I've done. But I don't want to hurt anyone else. I don't want to build a life with Joanna if I'm not strong enough to be there for her until the end." He buried his face in his hands. "Do you even exist? If you can hear me—give me some kind of sign. I just want to know what I'm supposed to do."

A loud knock on the outer door of Bradford's apartment had him instantly on his feet, gun drawn, and heading along the wall toward the entrance. No one knew where he lived.

Off to the side of the door, he stood perfectly still and waited.

"Bradford probably doesn't even live here," Dylan said in a loud voice. "I told you we should've called first."

Just as loud, Connor said, "Clay is never wrong about this stuff. Knock again. Maybe he's on the toilet."

Bradford holstered his gun and opened his door. "What the hell are you two doing here?"

They both walked past him, arms full of store boxes and bags. Once inside, Connor deposited the bags on the couch. "A little squirrel told us where you live."

Dylan corrected him as he deposited his packages next to Connor's. "It's supposed to be a birdie. A little birdie told us."

Connor made a face. "Does it really matter what fucking woodland creature I say told us? It's an expression."

"That's the thing about expressions. They're always the same. You say a man has balls of steel. Not balls of granite. They're the same thing, but one sounds weird."

"Hey, if you want to stand around and talk about men's balls being hard and think any version of that is not weird, more power to you." Connor tipped his head to one side and asked, "Why isn't saying a woman has a vagina of steel a thing?"

"First of all," Dylan countered, "it would be a pussy of steel and it just sounds unfuckable."

"But balls of steel are better?" Connor shook his head. "I prefer my balls just the way they are."

Bradford threw up two hands. "Now that we've cleared

that up can we get back to what that's all about?" He referenced the high pile of packages. "I won't even ask who told you this address because I would have to kill him."

"Clay—" Connor started to say, but Dylan elbowed him in the gut hard enough that he doubled over.

"You heard the man," Dylan said. "He doesn't want to know."

Connor put a hand on his side. "You are so lucky I'm too mature now to punch you in the head."

Dylan shrugged. "Too mature—or too much of a pussy—whatever."

"How many times are you going to work the word pussy into our conversation? And why? Oh, is it because I'm still having more sex than you are?"

Bradford tried to hold it back, but he gave in to a laugh. Dylan and Connor were entertaining on their own, but when they were together they were a fucking comedy show.

The two brothers stopped arguing and turned toward Bradford. Connor was the first to speak. "Don't be offended by what we're about to suggest."

Bradford folded his arms across his chest.

Dylan shifted from one foot to the other. "Connor and I completely understand. Neither of us thought we should have to change at all."

"But we gave it a try," Connor said, "and it turned out better than we thought."

"No." Bradford chose a tone that usually stopped even these meatheads in their tracks.

Connor walked over to the bags he'd placed on the

couch and pulled out several boxes. "Don't think of it as changing who you are, just softening your image."

Very few men would have not read Bradford's body language and tone as a threat, but Connor was like a Labrador who kept wagging its tail no matter how many times it was reprimanded. And Dylan? Bradford hadn't spent as much time with him, but he was a hell of a lot more likeable now that Joanna wasn't interested in him.

Dylan added, "What you're wearing now is already better than your usual hitman look."

"It's more than a look." Dylan's eyes widened and Bradford held back a smile. If Connor and Dylan were there to suggest he get a makeover, they deserved to be messed with.

"He's joking, Dylan." Connor laughed. In one hand he held up a pair of cowboy boots. "What do you think of these?" In his other hand he waved leather work boots. "Or these?"

Relaxing, Dylan said, "Hey, does it strike you as funny that we're here to teach the opposite of what Claire taught us? Remember when she made us stash our boots and promise not to wear them to any more events?"

Ian's wife was a life coach and had indeed morphed Dylan and Connor from redneck construction types to Hollywood heartthrobs. What the hell kind of change did they think Bradford required?

Connor pulled out a six-pack of beer and a cowboy hat. He placed the hat on his head. "I bought this for you, Bradford, but I kind of like how it looks on me."

"You should keep it," Bradford said in a dry voice.

"Toss me a beer, Connor," Dylan said. Connor threw a beer to his brother then one to Bradford.

Bradford cracked his open and took a long gulp. "As entertaining as it would be to see what else you wasted your money on, I have somewhere I need to be."

"Joanna awaits." Connor wiggled his eyebrows.

Bradford froze. "I've changed my mind. Before I lose my shit, tell me exactly what Clay told you."

Connor put the boots on the couch and pulled out another box. "Just that you have a date tonight with Joanna and you might need some help not messing it up. He gave us a credit card with no limit and released us in the city. Is it wrong that I enjoy spending his money?"

It wasn't. Clay had more than any person should. "That's it? That's why you're here?"

"That's all we needed to hear," Dylan said. "Joanna is the real deal. We'd love to see it work out between the two of you."

"Because?" Bradford challenged.

Dylan and Connor exchanged a look. Connor said, "Because we want you to be happy."

"This isn't about what *you* fucking want." Bradford growled then instantly regretted taking his frustration with himself out on them. "Thank you for wanting to help, but I've got everything under control."

"Do you?" Connor asked. "Show us your farm attire."

Bradford let his answer be his steady glare.

Dylan added, "Look at your shoes. Now those might be fine for a stakeout and might even be comfortable—"

"I'm not in law enforcement," Bradford cut in.

Dylan continued as if Bradford hadn't spoken. "—but you can't ride a horse in them."

"She rescues minis."

"Minis?" Dylan turned back toward Connor. "Why do we care what shoes he wears around them?"

Connor held up a blue plaid button-down shirt. *Plaid.* "We don't, but Joanna might. When people assess whether or not you fit in somewhere, their decision is in the details."

Dylan nodded. "Claire taught us that and it's true. Sometimes it's even subconscious." He waved a hand. "If you want to be accepted, it's important to look the part."

If Bradford hadn't known the amount of effort Connor and Dylan had put into fitting in with the Barringtons, he would have told them where they could stuff their ideas. They weren't there to judge Bradford, they were there to help in the only way they knew how. It was kind of sweet and made it harder to tell them to get the hell out of his apartment.

Connor threw the shirt at Bradford. "The important thing is to also remain true to yourself. Your mirrored glasses can stay. This is about expanding your wardrobe, not changing it."

Bradford held up the shirt he'd caught with his free hand. "I'm not the plaid type."

"But Joanna probably is and this is how you can show her you have more than one side to you," Connor said while digging through more of the packages. He held a box of condoms out for Bradford to take. "You probably have some, but since we were prepping for your big date we picked you up some. Never bought them for another man so we got the variety pack." When Bradford didn't reach for it, Connor put the box on the couch. "Anyway, now you don't have to worry about that."

Bradford started to relax as he chugged the rest of his beer. The meatheads were one of a kind. "Do I want to know what else you bought?"

Connor reached into another bag then hesitated before withdrawing the contents. "We debated whether or not this was crossing the line."

"I said it was," Dylan said.

"I said it was fine." Connor held out a pair of boxers covered with hearts. "Never underestimate the power of a good set of boxers. Imagine you find yourself in an argument with a woman and don't know how to tell her how you feel about her—reveal these and bam, she knows."

Dylan shook his head. "Bradford, never drop your pants in the middle of an argument. Worst advice ever. Tried it once, didn't help."

"Toss me another beer," Bradford said with a half groan, half laugh. He'd just imagined Dylan trying to impress a woman with a flashy set of underwear—it was an image he needed gone from his head.

Connor said, "I told you he'd love the boxers, Dylan."

Dylan shot Bradford a comically skeptical look. "Bradford, if that's your expression when you love something, we also need to work on your face."

This time Bradford gave into a full laugh.

Dylan backtracked a bit. "I didn't mean that the way it sounded."

Bradford tossed the shirt back to Connor and said, "We're good, Dylan."

Looking relieved, Dylan went to the couch and pulled out a bag of carrots. "This is what I thought you could use."

"Not bad. I will take those with me."

"You say that like the condoms were a bad idea." With a cocky look, Connor thumbed toward the couch. "They're always a good gift."

Dylan countered. "They wouldn't be at a funeral."

"What are you talking about?" Connor asked in an exasperated tone.

"Or a family reunion," Dylan said.

"Gross, Dylan." Connor made a face.

"Hey, you're the one who said they're always a good gift. I'm just suggesting that there are times when they wouldn't be appropriate."

Bradford tried to resist, but couldn't. He added, "Or a baby shower. Your kid is cute, but here, try not to have more."

Dylan laughed and pointed at him in recognition of hitting the target with that one. Connor smiled as well and said, "Whatever. Make a joke if you want, but you know you'll use them." He cupped a hand to one side of his mouth as if saying something in confidence. "Some glow in the dark."

"What's this?" Dylan picked up the swear jar Joanna had given Bradford.

"Put that down," Bradford growled more forcefully than

he'd meant to.

Dylan read the label before replacing the glass jar on the table. "A swear jar? Look at all the money in there already. Dude, forget what we said and run for your life. It's not worth it."

Connor stepped closer. "Stop, Dylan, he really likes her."

Bradford neither acknowledged nor denied that accusation.

"You do, don't you?" Dylan's mouth dropped open. "That's awesome. Except I stole her last night as my date. Sorry about that."

Bradford wanted to be irritated with him. It was still too easy to remember how Dylan had sat with his arm around Joanna's chair, but his big, goofy, apologetic smile made it impossible to not forgive him. "It's fine. You didn't know."

"Aha! You just admitted you like Joanna," Connor announced as if he'd just solved an unsolvable mystery.

"Can't get anything past you." There was no point denying it. A glance at his watch revealed he was running short of time. "Thank you for stopping by. I need to shower and change."

Connor downed the rest of his beer then put the can on the end table beside the couch, placing the plaid shirt beside it. "Come on, Dylan, our work here is done. Bradford, check out the rest of what we brought you. Don't be afraid to expand your comfort zone." He adjusted the cowboy hat on his head. "Are you okay with me keeping this?"

"It's where it belongs." Bradford walked over to the door and held it open. "Could the two of you do me a favor?"

"Sure," they both said as they cheerfully filed out into the hallway.

"Tell Clay if he ever tells anyone where I live again I will personally castrate him."

Connor shifted sideways as if to protect his own manhood. Dylan stepped back and said, "Will do. Though he probably has balls of gold. Golden balls. That reminds me of the meatball dish with the gravy."

"Swedish meatballs?" Connor asked.

"Yeah," Dylan said wistfully. "Now I'm hungry. Want to stop somewhere on the way home?"

"Sure," Connor replied, "I'll call Angelina. She and Whitney might want to meet us."

They were still talking while Bradford closed the door. He paused as he was walking by the swear jar. It could have been an offensive gift. It certainly was evidence that she wanted to change him. He glanced at the packages on the couch. *She's not the only one.*

Fucking Clay.

This morning was cool.

Sending the meatheads to my undisclosed apartment was sloppy and just the kind of careless move that gets someone like me killed.

And, oddly enough, I'm not looking to die today.

He picked up the swear jar and ran his thumb over the writing. Swears said in ecstasy were free. A grin spread across his face. He loved that she'd made this for him and how it reflected her sense of humor as well as her open sexuality.

She was a woman who knew what she wanted and for

some crazy reason she wanted him. Bradford replaced the jar and moved to the couch. He peered into one of the bags Dylan and Connor hadn't emptied. One had a bottle of wine and a skateboard. He wasn't sure he wanted to know what that combination was about. The next bag was full of snacks and socks.

Odd.

Useful.

He glanced upward. "Tell me the meatheads were not the sign I asked for. And what the hell am I supposed to do with a skateboard?"

There wasn't an answer from above and he hadn't expected one. He caught the plaid shirt out of the corner of his eye and picked it up again. He'd never worn plaid in his life. The color wasn't bad—deep blue. He dressed for a purpose rather than for vanity. His suit was a uniform that opened doors. Beyond that he really didn't care what he wore. If Joanna liked plaid there was no reason he couldn't wear it now and then.

He placed it on his bed beside his overnight bag, took a shower, dressed in that shirt and jeans then began to pack. Comb. Toothbrush. Toothpaste. Deodorant. Floss. Change of clothes. Socks—new ones thanks to Connor and Dylan. Wine. A few snacks. He stuffed the carrots in an outside pocket and almost left the skateboard behind, but since it fit he stuffed it into the center portion of the bag.

He almost sought out his own stash of condoms, but decided to fill a side pouch of the bag with some of the variety pack. They were good quality and maybe it was time he got a little adventurous with his protection.

As he zipped up his bag, he groaned and thought: *I can't believe I'm taking advice from the meatheads.*

He remembered the heart boxers and almost left them but then at the last minute stuffed them into another of the bag's side pockets. Not for an argument—but maybe for a laugh.

He almost slipped on his dress shoes, but decided to try on the work boots Connor had brought.

Comfortable. Better than what he'd worn while in the service.

He walked over to the mirror in his bedroom and took a long look. *I look like a fucking lumberjack. Is this really what Joanna wants?*

He shook his head and swung the overnight bag over his shoulder. *Swim trunks.* He almost went back to his closet for them, then remembered she'd said they were optional and decided against it.

I like optional.

He bent, clipped his gun to a strap on his leg that concealed it beneath his jeans, then headed out the door. On his way to the garage he texted Joanna that he was on his way.

Her response was almost immediate: **Fantastic, I'll jump in the shower.**

That was all it took for him to speed the whole way to her farm. He would have gotten there in record time, but he stopped at a pastry shop to pick up her favorite dessert.

Chapter Nine

FRESH FROM THE shower, hair blown out, light makeup applied, Joanna paced her bedroom in just a towel. She was nervous/excited. Time had flown too fast for her to be ready on time. She'd stopped at a grocery store on the way back to pick up the ingredients for meatless tacos. Her plan was something light and fun, but now that she was rushing around, still trying to decide what to wear, she was worried she'd chosen something she couldn't have prepared by the time he arrived.

Her phone rang. It was Angelina. Perfect! "Hey, mind reader. I need some advice. Lace thong on a second date—sexy or trashy?"

Angelina laughed. "And this is why I can never have my friends on speakerphone. Let me step out of the room so Whitney can't hear us."

"Yes, please," Joanna answered with a chuckle.

"Okay, we're safe. When were you going to tell me you have a date with Bradford tonight?"

"Um. Now?" Joanna sighed. "I know we tell each other everything, but there's been a lot of negative noise regarding

Bradford and I wanted to get to know him on my terms."

"Does that mean I shouldn't tell you I think you're rushing things if you're already choosing underwear with him in mind? And what do you mean second date?"

Joanna bit her bottom lip, wrinkled her nose, then said, "We've already had one and it was magical."

"What? Did I fall into a coma and wake up days later or did this happen since last night?"

"Clay Landon might have surprised Bradford and me with a romantic breakfast and a tent full of games."

"Holy shit. You need to tell me everything. No, hold on, we should merge Aly into this convo."

"You're right." *I wouldn't want to be left out of something like this.*

A moment later Aly said, "So, I heard you're already at the choosing which underwear to wear phase. And you've been on a date? Is your head spinning?"

"It is. This morning was amazing."

"Spill," Aly said with a smile in her voice. "I just had a client say she's running a few minutes late and I told my receptionist to hold all calls."

Joanna started with her disappointment when she'd discovered the restaurant was not only full but that Bradford hadn't shown up after all. She described walking out, seeing him standing there, and how it had felt like a scene at the end of a romantic comedy. She'd wanted to run and throw herself into his arms. "But I didn't because we weren't in that place yet."

"Yet?" Angelina echoed. "Just how good was Clay's surprise?"

Joanna weighed her question before answering. "The date was good before we discovered the tent. There's a whole other side to Bradford—he's also sweet. We were smiling, holding hands, talking like we'd known each other forever, and then we came across this enormous white tent like people have at expensive weddings."

She described how the first part had been the Glass Slipper and breakfast. As she tried to capture the essence of the Ball Room, she kept using the word magical—because that's how it had felt.

"You were really locked in?" Aly asked. "And that didn't make you nervous at all?"

Angelina chimed in. "Aly, are you completely missing the romance of this? Joanna has a fairy godfather—"

"Who manipulated the situation like they were puppets."

Joanna sat on the corner of her bed. "It wasn't like that, Aly. Clay wanted us to have time together, that's all."

"If you're okay with it, I'm okay with it," Aly said. "I'm not trying to be a downer, I just want you to keep at least one toe planted in reality. I like Clay, but he's doing this because he finds it entertaining. What happens if he decides watching the two of you crash and burn is more fun?"

"Wow," Angelina said, "and you used to accuse me of being the pessimistic one. Aly, let Joanna have this. She has you and me to watch her back."

"You're not exactly unbiased when it comes to Clay. I know he's done a lot for Connor, but—"

"Does there have to be a but?" Joanna broke in. "I trust

people until they give me a reason not to. I enjoyed this morning. I intend to enjoy tonight. Do we have to make things more complicated than that?"

Aly signed. "I guess not. Sorry, I just worry about you."

"I know." If they were in the same room, Joanna would have hugged her. "I love you for that, but I'm a big girl. I've got this." She stood again and walked over to her bureau. "What I don't have is a decision about what to wear. Although I'm sure he wouldn't complain if I met him at the door in a towel, I was hoping to be a little less obvious."

"What are your options? I only have a few minutes before I have to get ready too. Although my night won't be as exciting as yours. Whitney, Connor, and I are going out to dinner with Dylan tonight."

Joanna went to her bureau and took out a few pairs, laying them out so she could match up the bras with them. "I have this white satin set, but it looks a little bridal to me."

Angelina suggested, "You have good instincts, so they're a no. What else do you have?"

Despite the fact that neither of her friends could see them, Joanna held up the tiny red thong with matching sheer lace bra. She described them, then said, "If I were ten pounds lighter I'd feel more confident in this, but—"

"Oh, please," Aly said, "never let the scale determine your sexual confidence. You are healthy and muscular because you live an active lifestyle. That's better than being half your size and weak. Which pair makes you *feel* the sexiest?"

Joanna dug back into her drawer and pulled out a black

mesh teddy with strategically placed designs that by no means provided enough coverage to make it decent. She'd never worn it, but when she bought it she'd imagined wearing it under a power suit while negotiating her next book deal. No one would have seen it, but it was a striking piece. She stepped into it and let her towel fall.

At first all she saw in the mirror were her flaws, but she shook her head and stood straighter. *This is me. Those are my mother's generous hips and grandmother's freckles. Not much I can do about either. And that's okay.*

"You're right, Aly. I was thinking about what he'd like, but I have one that I've been dying to wear and it's perfect."

"That's the one, then!"

"It sure is," Joanna said as she looked at herself in the mirror. It was slimming while still revealing. Her confidence rose. "I think I'll wear regular jeans and a shirt over this. It's kind of fun to keep things tame until I choose to release the tiger."

Aly laughed. "The *tiger*?"

"It's been a while," Joanna defended. "I have some pent-up needs I'm hoping will get satisfied tonight."

"Oh, boy," Angelina said. "Don't break the man."

"I won't." Bradford didn't seem like the fragile type.

Aly added, "Be careful."

"Where would the fun be in that?" Joanna checked the time and rushed to say, "I'll call you both tomorrow. He'll be here soon and I'm nowhere near ready."

She rushed through getting dressed then paused while choosing what to put on her feet. She usually wore barn boots or sneakers. Neither felt right for dinner with Brad-ford.

Her dog barking outside told her she was out of time. Since his visit would likely start with a tour of her farm, she hopped into socks and tugged on her barn boots before stepping out her front door.

She was out of breath and a little frazzled by the time she was on the steps of her house, but her nerves faded away when he stepped out of his car. She'd never imagined him in plaid or work boots, but, man, he was hot in both. He stood behind the driver-side door of his car as if unsure if he was coming or going.

She nearly sprinted down the steps to greet him. "Wel-come to Treasures Farm."

He didn't smile and his sunglasses blocked her ability to read his mood. He was far from the first reluctant visitor to her farm, but most of them had four legs. More surprising, her normally rowdy golden retriever, Buddy, was sitting on the grass watching Bradford—from a respectful distance.

She made her way to Bradford's car. Was he afraid of dogs? It hadn't occurred to her to pen Buddy, but not everyone liked animals. The thought saddened Joanna. She could overlook many things but not that difference. "Buddy, come." Her dog sat where he was, wagging his tail and looking at Bradford. If Bradford had reprimanded him, it certainly hadn't been harshly. Buddy was a wimp. "Sorry, I should have put him away."

Bradford looked from her to Buddy and frowned. "He doesn't look like trouble."

She laughed. "Looks can be deceiving, but he's so loveable no one can stay mad at him."

"I brought a bag. Should I bring it in?" Bradford's tone was harsh and her heart melted. He was nervous.

"Why don't we put it inside the front door then I'll give you a tour of the farm—if you'd like."

"Sounds good." He pulled a large black bag out of the back of his car.

"Looks like you're moving in," she joked then wished she hadn't when he visibly tensed. "That's a joke, Bradford. You can laugh."

Bradford swung his bag over his shoulder, an act that highlighted a mouth-watering amount of muscle. God, he looked good in jeans.

She stepped closer. "Is everything okay, Bradford? Talk to me."

He didn't say anything for a moment, then he removed his sunglasses and looked into her eyes. She held her breath, waiting. There was so much emotion in his eyes, she wished he would just let it out. Was he worried it would overwhelm her? It wouldn't. She had all kinds of feelings swirling around in her as well. "There's something for you on the passenger seat."

It wasn't the declaration she'd expected, but when she spotted a cake box on the car seat, warmth spread through her. He was so gruff on the outside, but considerate and sweet beneath that. "Thank you." She retrieved the box and smiled at him.

"It's strawberry shortcake."

Her eyes rounded as she returned to his side. "That's my favorite. How did you know?" When he didn't answer she decided that was a story for later. "Well, I love it. Thank you."

He cleared his throat. "I also brought carrots for your horses." He swung the bag forward. He opened an outside pouch of his bag then rezipped it quickly. Was it her imagination or did his cheeks flush? He unzipped another pouch and pulled out a bag of organic carrots.

Other men had brought her flowers. Some had bought her expensive jewelry, something that had always left her feeling a little uncomfortable, especially when it was early in their relationship. No one had ever brought her carrots and cake.

She accepted the carrots. With one of his gifts in each hand she went up onto her toes and kissed his lips, slowly and gently as her thank you.

His mouth moved over hers with the same hunger she was fighting. His free hand pulled her against him, his hardening cock making it intoxicatingly clear that the kiss was exciting him as much as it was her. When she broke off the kiss, she stayed close enough to him that she could feel the heat of his body. Every inch of her was humming for him.

Joanna had only been with a handful of men in her life. She tended to ease into a relationship slowly, become friends before becoming lovers—but her body had different ideas when it came to Bradford. It argued there would be time later to get to know everything about him. That burning need was what made Joanna bolder than she'd ever been with a man. "I'm glad you're here."

His smile was reflected in his eyes. "Me too."

"Let's go put your stuff inside." She started to move toward the house and he fell into step beside her. Buddy joined them, choosing to walk at Bradford's side. She gave him a curious look. "Do you have a dog, Bradford?"

"No."

"Ever had one?"

"No, why? Because your dog likes me?"

When they reached the door and stopped, Buddy sat beside Bradford like the trainers had attempted and failed to teach him to do for them. "No, because he respects you. He was supposed to be a therapy dog, but he failed puppy discipline school—twice. I often have to pen him because he is too enthusiastic when he first meets people. I've never seen him as well-behaved as he is right now."

Bradford looked down at Buddy. The dog gazed up at him with his tongue hanging out, his tail wagging, but his butt planted firmly on the porch floor.

"Dogs get me," Bradford said casually, dismissing a gift that another person might have bragged about.

She wanted to ask him what he thought Buddy got about him, but she didn't think Bradford was ready for that conversation yet. Her take on animals was that they were a good read of character. They filtered out what people said and judged them by body language and behavior. Nothing about Bradford was threatening, but he quietly commanded respect.

Joanna was beginning to get Bradford. She guessed this was all new territory for him as well, but he was trying. She placed the bag of carrots near the door. "I'll put the dessert in the kitchen and come right back. You can put your bag inside. There's a bathroom down the hall on the left if you need one."

He followed her and placed his bag against the wall just inside. "All set. I'll meet you on the porch."

After putting the strawberry shortcake in the fridge, Joanna headed back to meet Bradford, but stopped before pushing the screen door open. Bradford was sitting on the steps with a smitten Buddy at his side. *I like him too, Buddy.*

She thought of other men who'd met Buddy. Some had made a big show of loving him up. Some had thrown a ball for him and actively tried to build a relationship with him. Funny how effortless Bradford made their connection look.

Bradford stood and turned at the sound of her opening the door. He had a funny look in his eyes, like he was holding back something he wanted to say. "Joanna—"

"Yes?"

He paused, then said, "Don't forget the carrots."

She didn't spare them a look, instead she walked over to him, ran her hands up his chest and said, "What carrots?"

"Don't." He caught her hands and growled. "I'm trying to do this right."

She froze. "Are you implying I'm doing it wrong?" So much for being a femme fatal. Embarrassment began to sweep through her. She tried to pull her hands free.

His grip on them tightened. "No. Not at all. Sorry, my

ability to speak goes to shit around you." He expelled a harsh breath. "You matter to me more than anyone has in a long time. I don't know how that's supposed to change things. I don't want you to think I'm only here because—"

She put a hand over his lips. "I don't. We're quite a pair, aren't we? I make you stop and think and you make me want to be impulsive."

After a brief silence, he muttered, "I'm fucking this up."

She shifted closer and wrapped her arms around him. "No, you're convincing me that my instincts about you are right. You're a good man, Bradford. I know you've done some things you believe are unforgivable, but I don't see any of that when I look at you. All I see is a man who cares more about the welfare of others than himself."

He laid his head against the side of hers and breathed her in. "How impulsive?"

"That's all you got out of what I said?" She smiled against his rock-hard chest. Without waiting for a response, she said, "If I were a stronger woman or you were a smaller man, I'd toss you over my shoulder and haul you off to my bed."

He chuckled. "That's quite an image, but I prefer to do the carrying." He bent and lifted her in his arms. "I told myself I'd take it slow with you." He opened the door, carried her inside, then kicked the door closed behind him. "If I walk to your bedroom, really slowly, does that count?"

She laughed from the pleasure of being carried, the fun of discovering Bradford had a sense of humor beneath his growl, and the excitement of being with a man who made her feel young and reckless. "I'll check the rulebook, but I think it does."

He kissed her and all joking fell to the wayside. There was only him, his mouth teasing hers to open, and a need to strip away the clothing separating them. They didn't make it far into her house before he must have felt the same way because he lowered her to her feet. He broke off the kiss just long enough to pull her T-shirt up and over her head.

The desire in his eyes when he took in the top of her sheer black bodysuit was all she could have hoped for. She'd never felt sexier nor wanted a man more. He didn't have to tell her how beautiful he found her, it was right there in his smile as he traced her curves through the thin material.

He stripped her down to just the bodysuit. His heated gaze told her more than any man ever had with words. This was real. It was primal and undeniable.

When she reached for his shirt, he stilled her hands and said, "I want to enjoy you first."

Joanna doubted there was a woman who would have denied his request. He turned her before him, kissing his way along each part of her as he went. His hands were everywhere—strong and confident. When he slid the bodysuit straps over her shoulders and down her arms she was too turned on to be embarrassed by being fully undressed before a man who was still in his clothing. As he dropped the bodysuit to the floor, he said, "Beautiful, but this is better."

Well now I know where I can save money. I could have worn my grannie panties and I doubt he would have noticed.

He took a moment to look her over again and liked what

he saw if the huge bulge in the front of his jeans was anything to go by. He slid a hand down her stomach and dipped a finger between her folds. There was no fumbling, no question he knew how to bring a woman pleasure. He gently began to move a finger back and forth over her clit while bending to kiss her breasts.

She spread her legs wider for him and was rewarded by one of his fingers sliding inside. She reached for his belt, but he shifted his hips away and murmured, "Look at me. When you come I want to see it in your eyes."

His commands were followed by his teeth gently grazing over her nipples. He plunged a second finger in her, somehow continuing the back and forth motion over her clit. Her body felt like an instrument he was playing with rare talent. Nothing was rushed. The rhythm he created with his hand became one that echoed through her.

In and out.

Back and forth.

Even his kisses came with precision. He had a method to his madness and it was a delicious assault. One breast then the other. Her neck. Her shoulders. The place right behind her ear she hadn't known would drive her crazy.

In and out faster.

Back and forth harder.

A nip that didn't hurt.

He withdrew his hand and carried her into her living room and sat her on the thick back of her couch. She was afraid she might fall off, but he was down on his knees in front of her, pulling her forward so her legs draped over his shoulders and her ass was supported by his hands while her back remained on the couch. The position stretched her sex wide before his mouth.

His breath was its own caress.

Then his tongue.

Oh, God, that tongue.

He ran it between her folds, before using one hand to open her more. He teased her with the tip of his tongue, drove his tongue deeper inside her than she would have thought possible, then returned to flick her clit with a speed that drove her wild.

He moved his hand so he could insert a finger inside her while still working magic with his tongue. She shifted and slipped, no longer holding herself up—she was at his mercy. She let go of the fear of where she was, let herself trust that he'd take care of her, and gave herself over to the pleasure building within her.

Her head fell back and she closed her eyes as she approached what was promised to be an amazing orgasm. He withdrew and her eyes flew open. She adjusted her position so she was once again steady and watched him undo his belt, unzip the front of his jeans and release a mouth-watering cock. He held her gaze while he sheathed himself in a condom.

She'd never had sex with someone who was still dressed but there was something incredibly hot about it. He was taking her on his terms.

He picked her up, this time wrapping her legs around his waist. Their kiss was deep, hot. She clung to his shoulders and cried out with pleasure when his first thrust was deep and sure. So big. So hard. He made no excuses nor accommodations for his size. She stretched wide to accept him and loved when his second thrust was just as powerful and deep. "Oh, yes," she whispered against his lips.

He used the back of the couch for leverage and pounded into her, each time harder, faster, deeper. Their kiss was a wonderfully feverish claiming as well. When she closed her eyes, he growled for her to open them, like she was his to command.

And she was.

She'd never been with a man of his size and strength. It was exciting in an out-of-control way. His touch became rough—hers did as well. She couldn't get enough of him, give him enough of herself.

When she came she was looking into his eyes, calling out his name, clenching her sex tightly around his shaft. His face tightened and with a few final deep thrusts, he came as well.

She collapsed against his still-clothed chest and he held her there for several long moments before withdrawing from her and easing her back to her feet. He cleaned himself off, disposed of the condom, and was back with her while she was still enjoying her post-orgasm bliss.

When he joined her, she stepped into his arms. Shifting her hips back and forth so her sex grazed the growing bulge in his jeans, she sighed. "That was amazing."

"It was."

She ran her other hand down his neck and over the buttons of his shirt. "I'm up for another round if you are." She cupped his hardening cock through his jeans. "But this time lose the clothes."

He tensed against her.

Her hands stilled. "What's wrong?"

NOTHING SHOULD BE wrong. That's what Bradford told himself. He'd just fucked the most incredible woman he'd ever met and she was eager for more. He should be stripping off his clothing without hesitation.

He wasn't a vain man, but he didn't want her to see him yet. It wasn't like he normally kept his clothes on when he fucked someone, but Joanna was different. The women he was usually with thought his scars were cool. A lot of women liked to fuck men they considered dangerous and his scars added to their fantasy.

Joanna would ask questions he didn't want to answer. Rather than be impressed, she'd understand that each one had cost him something—broken him a little more. The last thing he wanted to see in her eyes was pity.

He let his hands fall away from her and stepped back. She moved closer and put a hand on his chest. "Take me with you," she said.

"I'm not going anywhere," he said in a harsh tone.

With her other hand she touched his temple. "Up here. Whatever you're thinking, share it with me."

He took her hand in his, brought it to his mouth, and kissed it. Had she gotten defensive he would have pulled farther away. "Why do you have to be so damned understanding?"

She didn't seem bothered by his question. Instead she traced his jaw with her free hand. "You shouldn't have sex with someone you don't trust."

He frowned. "I trust you." Well, as much as he trusted anyone.

"Then don't shut me out. Are you self-conscious?"

"No."

"Infectious?"

He laughed without humor and said, "Definitely not."

"Then what is it? I'm standing here buck naked and ten pounds overweight, and I'm not worried about it. Do you have a thing where you can only have sex while dressed?"

"No." He stepped back and rubbed his hands over his face. "But this is different."

"Bradford?"

"Yes?"

"Just fucking tell me. It can't be as bad as all the things I'm thinking."

A smile pulled at one side of his mouth. "Since when do you swear?"

When she put her hands on her hips, an action that bounced both of her breasts, he almost forgot what the problem was. "I swear, just not much. You, however, are bringing it out in me right now. And you're killing my post-orgasm buzz."

He came to a decision then. "I don't want to do that."

She ran her hands up his chest. "No, you don't. So, speak. Most things seem worse in our heads than they are when we say them aloud."

He loved the feel of her. From the delicate back of her neck to the roundness of her ass—she was perfection. "You may be right."

Her eyes lit up. "Those are my favorite words."

He chuckled then sobered. "I don't want to hear what I know you'll say, but I don't want to hurt your feelings by telling you to keep it to yourself."

"Okay. I need a moment to unpack that, but I think I understand what you're saying. I would never intentionally say anything to hurt your feelings, Bradford."

"This isn't about hurting my feelings." He began to unbutton his shirt. "Don't even say anything with your eyes."

"Got it. Even my eyes will be silent."

He dropped his shirt to the floor. To give her credit her expression remained the same even as she took in the scars on his chest. When he turned so she could see his back, though, she gasped.

"Oh, my God, Bradford." There it was—the pained sympathy for him. He didn't want it. The scars from the chain beating he'd received in his teens only caused him pain when he remembered the circumstances surrounding them. To him, they represented a failure he'd never quite been able to reconcile.

He picked up his shirt and slid his arms back into it. "Don't ask about them."

She hugged him close, skin to skin, with all the open affection she'd shown him earlier that day. "I won't."

He stood there, stiff as a board in her embrace, until he once again drove back the memories of his sister and the people who had taken everything from him. Killing them hadn't brought him the peace he'd hoped it would.

The tighter she held him, the worse he felt. He could live with the weight of the past, but he couldn't endure a moment of hurting her. Was she already regretting having sex with him?

"I'm sorry," he said.

She raised her head. "Don't be. You've done nothing wrong."

"I wish that were true." He settled her against his chest, tucking her beneath his chin. He thought about her grandfather. He'd wanted to protect his wife from his darker side and what had that brought them? "If I tell you a story it's not because I want your sympathy. In fact, that's the last thing I want. But you deserve to know the truth about me and why I am the way I am."

"Okay," she murmured against his chest.

He went back to the beginning, although he'd already told her about his parents. She needed context for his actions. He told her about how losing his parents had separated him from his sister. He outlined the series of choices she'd made that put her at the mercy of the same gang that had killed their parents. Without emotion he described his first attempt to rescue her and the warning beating he'd received. His voice deepened as he shared how he'd gone back, even more determined that he could save his sister, only to fail again. The beating that had left him with a severely scarred back, a disfigured face, and a bullet that was still lodged somewhere within him. "They left me for dead because I should have been dead. No one survives what they did to me, but I did. For a long time I was angry about that. Why keep me here when everything I cared about was gone? My foster father encouraged me to join the Army and I did, but I was an empty shell—until I saw a news clip about one of the gang members who'd pimped out my sister. He was still alive and still pimping women out. I knew then that I'd been spared for a purpose. I killed him, Joanna. I killed every last one of the men who hurt my sister. Then I went on to find other people who were hurting the vulnerable, and I killed them too."

She shuddered against him. "That sounds like a lot of people."

"It was."

"Are you ever afraid of being caught?"

He shook his head. "By now what I've done isn't exactly a secret—not to those who watch everything everyone does. I've been a necessary evil though. And I have some powerful friends."

"You and Ian."

"Yes. Like I've said before, I'm the one the government calls when something can't be handled via normal channels. I'm too useful to too many important people to ever be held accountable for how it started."

"And when you're no longer useful to them?"

"I have enough dirt on almost everyone that only a fool would come for me."

She tipped her head back to meet his gaze. "Do you have dirt on me?"

He decided to lighten the mood. "Yep. You talk too much during sex."

Her eyes widened. "What? I barely said a word."

He mimicked a mouth with his hand, opening and closing it. "We could already be having sex for a second time, but there you go—still yip-yapping."

"Oh, really? Well here is something for your research. I'm also a gifted pincher." She twisted a small bit of skin on his side.

He laughed and caught her hand. "Stop that. It tickles."

"So, you're ticklish? There you go, just handing me an advantage I wasn't even looking for." She gave his sides a playful tweak.

He laughed more and twisted to avoid her fingers. "Okay. Okay. Stop."

She kept her fingers poised. "I will if you promise me something."

Still laughing, he said, "Sure. Whatever."

"When I'm naked, you're naked."

He studied her expression, looked deeply into her eyes, and didn't see the pity he'd been afraid to see. Instead he saw humor, desire, and confidence.

The plaid shirt hit the floor again. His boots, pants, boxers, and socks followed. He removed his calf gun holster and put it, as well as the gun, on the table.

"Hang on, you were wearing a gun while we had sex?"

He used his hand to mimic a mouth talking again and she pretended to tickle him again. Humor was replaced by heat when one of her hands circled his cock while her other hand cupped his balls. "Joanna."

Her hands stilled. "Yes?"

He ran a hand through her hair and imagined her mouth replacing her hands. He didn't believe in telepathy, but he didn't not believe in it either when she sank to her knees and those beautiful lips of hers wrapped around his cock. His hand fisted in her hair as her tongue circled his tip. He urged her to take him deeper. She didn't. She withdrew slightly and kissed the tip of his dick, then licked the underside from base to tip. Her tongue flicked back and forth just below the head of his cock before she took him into her mouth again, slowly this time. Her breath had him throbbing with anticipation, ready to beg her to take him deeper.

Her mouth alone would have been enough, but her fingers were working their own magic. She massaged his balls as her thumb caressed circles behind them, making him wonder, while also not wanting to know, where the hell she learned to do that. It was fucking incredible.

She took her time, pausing to kiss his thighs, his stomach, then lick her way up and down his shaft before taking it back into her mouth again. Slowly, skillfully, she brought him to the edge of an orgasm and stopped.

She rose to her feet, turned around, and bent over the arm of the couch. He sheathed himself then kissed his way up and down her back. He lightly kicked her legs farther apart and took his time kissing his way down that beautiful ass of hers right back up to her neck.

He slowly slid inside her, making sure she was ready for him, and held her hips to control their rhythm. He moved in and out, teasing her as she had him. Her sex was wet and ready but he wanted more for her so he reached around and laved her clit while he kept his thrusts slow and easy.

Releasing her hips, he sought out her gorgeous tits and gently pinched their excited nubs between his thumb and finger. She begged him not to stop so he didn't.

He explored her body, seeking out what drove her most wild, all the while keeping his thrusts deep and slow. When her breathing became quicker and she began to moan and writhe against his hand he brought his hands back to her hips and began to pound into her.

There was no gentleness in him and no request for some from her. "I'm coming," she called out with a shudder. He kept his rhythm, but held back.

When she sighed he turned her around and walked with her in his arms until her back was against the wall. Her legs wound around his hips, opening her for him again. He slammed into her, again and again, fucking her mouth with his tongue while driving himself deeper and deeper into her.

She whimpered and he raised his head, worried he might have been too rough. She dragged his mouth back to hers, saying, "Don't stop. Don't you dare fucking stop. I'm going to come again."

It was a demand he had no issue following. Their tongues intertwined again and he let the last of his control go, loving that she liked it as rough as he did. God, she was perfect.

Chapter Ten

IT HAD TAKEN just a suggestion of post-sex skinny-dipping for Joanna and Bradford to end up in her pool. Although her property bustled during the day with visitors, she'd made it clear that it was also her home. Aly and Angelina tended to think Joanna was a pushover but she wasn't—not when it came to things that mattered.

Treasures Farm was a life passion and she ran it with strict policies because the animals she took in depended on her. Compassion—to be worthwhile—needed to be followed with meaningful action.

Joanna had her arms draped over a pool float as Bradford did laps. She would have encouraged him to relax and join her but she was enjoying the view too much. His technique was different from how most people swam. He kicked off the wall of the pool but stayed on the surface with his face underwater. Rather than use his arms to swim, he kept them together in front of him or flush at his sides. Every now and then he would roll to one side to catch a breath. Her pool was long but he made it across with very little effort.

She shamelessly enjoyed watching him. He was all mus-cle and looked more at home in the water than she would have guessed. The scars on his back still pained her, but the shock of them had passed. She would have loved to ask him about each of his tattoos, but she understood the value of patience.

Every creature came around on their own schedule, but the process for reaching them was the same—consistency and kindness. Bradford had trust issues, but after hearing about his childhood she understood why. She didn't like the idea of killing anything, human or animal, but she wasn't naive when it came to the existence of evil in the world.

What would I do to someone who killed my parents? Someone who hurt my sister, if I had one, and was the reason for her death as well? If I knew they were out there still hurting others and no one else could stop them?

I don't know what I would do in that case.

She thought about the other situations he'd shared with her. *If someone had my child? If they'd already killed and I was confident they'd kill mine as well? Could I take that person's life?*

I think I could.

How would I see someone like Bradford? Someone who came in, killed the kidnapper, and returned my child?

He would forever be a hero in my heart.

Bradford doesn't see himself in that light.

Her heart broke for the young man who had tried and failed to save his sister. He'd said it scared him when he enjoyed taking a criminal out. *I can understand that too. No hero wants to become what he's fighting against.*

My grandfather feared he had.

Bradford went back and forth across the pool without seeming to tire. *He pushes himself. Does he hate himself the way my grandfather did?*

Do I have what it takes to help him if he does?

As if sensing her thoughts were headed down a dark path, Bradford ended his last lap by returning to her. "I haven't had a swim for pleasure in a long time. This was a great idea."

She wiggled her eyebrows. "The pleasure was all mine."

He moved to where he could stand and pulled her into the circle of his arms. She slid along his muscular thighs and moaned her approval. Gently, he traced the side of her face with the back of his hand. "How did any man ever let you go?"

She wrapped her legs around his waist for balance. "It's usually me who breaks it off."

He leisurely cupped one of her breasts. "Because?"

She didn't want to talk about other men with him, but he'd shared so much with her she felt she owed him the truth. "I don't want to settle. I've been with people I could imagine living with, but I've never found anyone I couldn't imagine living without."

He looked down into her eyes. "That's what you were hoping to find with Dylan?"

She frowned. "It's what I'm always looking for. That being said, I believe in giving people a chance. In order to really know someone you have to put in the time. I don't regret any of my past relationships even if they didn't work out. We tried."

"So that's what you're doing . . . giving us a try?"

She wasn't sure what he was looking for her to say, but she believed a person couldn't go wrong with honesty. "That's all we can do. You might discover you prefer a woman who smells a little less like horse all the time. I might—" She stopped there, not sure if they were at that level of truth yet.

"I prefer horse over perfume." His hands slid down her back to her bare ass. "What would your deal breaker be?"

She decided to just say it. She ran her hands up his chest and down his strong arms. "If you released any of your anger on me or anyone in my life. Treasures Farm is a place where feeling safe is priority one for everyone and every creature."

His hands tightened on her ass. "I would never hurt you."

"I would never let you." She gripped his shoulders. It was an uncomfortable conversation, but one that once begun needed to be completed. "I don't believe you would hurt me, but you asked the question and that's my answer. You're a good man, but you've been through more than any person should. To be in my life you can't let your pain be an excuse to hurt those around you. That would be my deal breaker. How about you?"

Without hesitation he answered, "If I ever thought I couldn't keep you safe."

She fell a little bit in love with him right then. He hadn't said the words with bravado or even to win her over. They were simply how he felt.

She gave him a slippery, full-body hug that included a kiss she hoped expressed how she felt. He spun her around, his cock coming to attention beneath the water. At the same time, her stomach rumbled and she remembered something. "I have a confession."

He froze but didn't say anything, just looked down at

her and waited.

She wrinkled her nose. "I never made dinner. How do you feel about cereal?"

His expression didn't change for a moment, then a smile spread across his face. "Is it a brand of cereal that one might serve naked?"

"Always," she answered with a wink.

"Then I'm starving." He started to walk into the shallow end of the pool with her still wrapped around him.

She held on tighter as he carried her up the steps and toward the house. "I've heard this brand is best served in bed and shared."

He stopped on the back porch of her house and lowered her to her feet. "I'll take my bag to your bedroom."

"I'll get the cereal."

He gave her a curious look. "I have glow in the dark condoms and boxers with hearts on them."

Joanna burst out laughing. "Sounds like a wild party to me."

He laughed along and gave her ass a swat. She opened the door, held it for him to walk through, and gave his naked ass a swat as well.

They'd had some heavy conversations that day, shared more than she would have imagined this early on, and returned to a playful place.

She was hopeful.

Hungry.

And ready for round three.

Not a bad second date. Not bad at all.

Chapter Eleven

I T WAS JUST after three in the morning when Bradford barely contained an angry scream and sat straight up in Joanna's bed. He was in a full sweat and breathing like he'd just run a 10K. Worst of all, he remembered his dreams this time.

His traitorous subconscious had just shown him endless ways he could put Joanna at risk and every single time he failed her. Every fucking time.

She was shot running for cover. She drowned jumping from a boat set to explode. He saw her tortured as he'd been, raped repeatedly, sold into the sex trade. No matter what he did, he couldn't save her. Just before he woke she'd been about to inject herself with a drug one of her captors told her would take her pain away. He'd screamed for her to stop, begged her to drop the needle and come to him, but she merely looked at him sadly and brought the needle up to her arm.

He bent over in the bed and gasped for air, doing his best to push the images out of his head. Joanna turned on a light beside the bed and put an arm around him. He hated that he was still shaking. He didn't want any part of what was in his head to affect her.

She didn't speak for a long time. Even though he didn't return her embrace, she continued to simply hold him. He took several deep breaths and slowly brought his body back under control. In a guttural tone, he said, "Sorry I woke you."

She simply hugged him tighter. "Yeah, you're a real asshole."

He smiled and brought an arm around her. "This is why I don't normally spend the night with anyone."

She brought a hand up to his scarred cheek. "Thank you for trusting me enough to let me see it."

He turned his face so he could kiss her hand. "I'm fucked up, Joanna. Maybe too much."

She wiped a tear from one of her cheeks. "I don't believe that, but I do think if you have something that you can't handle on your own there is no shame seeking out a professional—or a priest."

He shook his head. "Too much of what's in my head is classified and would endanger people's lives if it got out." He rubbed a hand over his face. "It would almost be worth it to see the expression on a priest's face if I let it all out on him." He glanced down at Joanna. "I'd have to kill him though, for the safety of others, so how much would that help?"

She tensed, scanned his face, then relaxed. "That's not funny."

He took another deep breath and acknowledged his attempt at lightening the mood might have been too dark to be effective. He pinched the air in front of his face. "Not even a little?"

She rolled her eyes then settled against him again. "Do you want to talk about your dream?"

"Not really."

For several moments neither of them said anything. Her presence was both a comfort and a reminder of his nightmare. "Have you ever done drugs?"

"No. You?"

"Never. Don't take them. Even if they make you feel good in the moment, they will destroy your life."

"I have no plans of experimenting with drugs, but okay."

He took another deep breath. "Don't believe anyone you don't know well who says I sent them to get you. I would never do that. If I couldn't make it to you, I would send Ian or Connor. Possibly the Barringtons. Maybe Aly or Angelina."

"Ooo-kay."

"Do you know how to swim well? If not, I could teach you."

"I'm a good swimmer." She tipped her head to the side. "Bradford, what is this about?" When he didn't answer, she asked, "Did you dream about something happening to me?"

He shuddered. "I can't be the reason you get hurt."

"You won't be."

He turned and looked her in the eye. "If we do this—if we give us a real try—you'll always need to be careful. Is being with me worth it?"

Holding his gaze without blinking, she answered, "Yes."

He pulled her across his lap and hugged her to him, burying his face in her hair. "I did not know it was possible to feel so good and so bad at the same time. The biggest favor I could do for you would be to walk away and not look back, but I can't. Staying is selfish and dangerous, but I don't want to be anywhere but here."

She ran a comforting hand back and forth across his chest. "You should definitely talk to someone, but I understand what you're saying about the sensitive nature of what you need to get out. You know who has never spilled a single secret I've ever shared with her? Betty."

"Betty, your rescue horse?"

"She's a very good listener."

He kissed the top of Joanna's head. "Thanks, but no." If he got to the point where he needed to unload his issues on a miniature horse, he might as well cash in his chips right then. "Three o'clock is a tough hour for me."

Joanna's mouth rounded. "Is that—Was that when—"

"Yes, that's my sister's time of death on the coroner's report."

"I'm so sorry."

"It's not always this bad."

"What do you do when it is?"

"I usually go for a run."

"Well, I'm wide awake so would you consider a walk instead? I didn't check the barn before we went to bed. It's dark, but I can still show you around."

"I'd like that."

She stood and began to dress. "Depending on how long

we're out there, we might as well feed and clean the stalls. Good news? I told my help to stay home this morning so we could be alone. Bad news, no one will be here until around ten to help out."

It all sounded good to him. He rose and began to dress as well. "How many horses do you have?"

"Wait, do you *not* know?"

"Nine. One you've had for years, Betty, and the rest are here for training before heading off to the Seeing Horse Foundation or any of the horse therapy organizations you're affiliated with."

Pausing just before putting a shirt on, she said, "These background checks of yours seem quite detailed."

A guilty smile curled his lips. "I may have found you and what you do fascinating."

That brought a smile to her face as well. She put on her shirt then moved to sit on the bed to pull on socks as well. "It's a little unfair that you know so much about me before I know that much about you, but I'll take it as a compliment."

"I don't normally tell anyone what I know about them. It tends to creep people out."

She stood. "I could see that happening. I don't have anything to hide so I don't really care, but if you have uncovered anything about my parents there's no need to tell them when you meet them."

He looked up from tucking in his shirt. "Why would I meet your parents?"

"They're a big part of my life. If you spend much time with me you're bound to run into them."

"Oh."

She wrinkled her nose at him. "Don't worry, it's not like it's going to happen any time soon. And if it does, just be yourself. My parents are laid back like me, but my father might still think I'm a virgin."

Bradford coughed.

Joanna arched an eyebrow. "I said *might*."

He laughed.

She joined in then added, "You know what? Just for that, I'm going to pretend I have no idea what to do the next time we have sex." She rounded her eyes and feigned fear. "Is that a p-p-penis? I've never seen one before, can't even say the word."

He closed the distance between them and looped his arms around her waist, pulling her flush against him. "I have no desire to imagine you with another man, but I also have no complaints."

She arched her back so she could look up at him. "We don't need to talk about our exes. I don't like imagining you with anyone else either."

He kissed her and let the passion that welled up between them be his promise. When he raised his head, he took an extra moment to simply appreciate the beauty of her flushed face. "If we're going for a walk we should go . . ."

"Yeah, we definitely need to pace ourselves. One more orgasm and I may lose my ability to speak. I'm so freaking relaxed."

He shifted her against his arousing cock. "Wait, you didn't tell me silence was a possible outcome. If more women offered that I guarantee men would be better fucks."

"Don't make me kick your ass." She smacked his chest lightly.

He bent and murmured in her ear, "Could you do it without talking?"

"I can do this without saying a word." With lightning speed Joanna brought her hands to his sides and started tickling. Things quickly evolved into a playful skirmish he could have easily won had he wanted to. He thought about the deal breaker she'd shared earlier and knew it wouldn't be an issue. He would never hurt a woman, and anyone or anything Joanna cared about was now under his protection. With a laugh he conceded defeat and her hands moved up behind his neck.

"Do you really think I talk too much?" she asked.

Just to bust her chops, he said, "That's an unfair question to ask while you have your hands around my throat."

"And that wasn't an answer." She looked skyward. "Not that I'm worried because I am who I am. Love me or hate me, this is me."

"I don't hate you."

Love? He'd never imagined feeling that was a possibility for him. It wasn't a description for how he felt yet, but if there ever was a woman he could imagine spending the rest of his life with, it was Joanna.

He joked about her talking too much, but the reality was he'd shared more with her than he ever had with anyone else. *So, really, the joke is about me and how all she has to do is look at me and I start vomiting my life's story to her.*

"Those chores you mentioned, could they wait an hour or so?"

She tipped her head to the side. "The horses would probably prefer it. At this time of day they're still sleeping."

He pulled his shirt up and over his head.

She did the same, dropping her bra on it without looking away from Bradford.

They both stepped out of the rest of their clothing pretty much in unison. She was so damned beautiful he was the one who was at a loss for words. "Don't change a single thing about yourself—not for me, not for anyone."

They exchanged a serious look that she softened by saying, "Why, sir, are you flattering me in hopes that I will have sex with you?"

He grinned at her. "Guilty as charged."

She raised a hand. "There's a real possibility it could happen, but I'll race you to the shower. First one there is the only one allowed to speak until we both orgasm again." She bent like a runner at a starting line.

Being with her was like nothing he'd dared hope for. He felt lighter—happy, even. He copied her stance. "You're on."

Of course, he let her win. He was done talking. He had better ideas for what to do with his mouth.

Chapter Twelve

*G*REAT SEX IS *exhausting.*

Chores started much later than normal, but only because cuddling naked in Bradford's arms was Joanna's newest favorite place to be. She took a break from cleaning a stall to watch Bradford finish one and move on to another without hesitation. *How is he not tired?* The man was a machine—a big, beefy, deliciously muscled and oh-so-talented-with-his-mouth machine.

I do this every day and I thought I was good, but he's done double the number of stalls I have.

As if sensing her attention, he looked over at her. The smile he gave her made her want to drop her pick and throw herself in his arms. There was too much to do, but that didn't stop her from indulging in a quick fantasy of another naked cuddle. She nodded toward the wheelbarrow of horse manure behind him. "You're a natural."

"I've always enjoyed manual labor. Clears my head."

She nodded. "People who don't have horses think I'm nuts when I say starting and ending my day like this makes me happy. It's when I organize my thoughts or shed the stress of the day. Some people do yoga—I clean stalls and paddocks."

"Doesn't sound crazy at all to me. We live complicated lives but the things that make people the most happy are usually the simplest of things. I often go for early morning runs. There's a quiet before the sun rises that isn't there the rest of the day."

"That's beautiful." The more time Joanna spent with Bradford the more she found to like about him. That wasn't the case with most people. Buddy padded down the aisle of the barn and wagged his tail when he saw Bradford. "What did you say to my dog that has him following you around like you're his?"

"I don't talk to canines," Bradford said. At the sound of Bradford's voice, Buddy did his excited dance that was often followed by him jumping up on a person. Joanna watched with fascination as Bradford shook his head almost imperceptibly. Buddy went down in a playful stance, front feet stretched forward, tail wagging wildly. Bradford pointed toward the ground and Buddy sat.

Joanna almost called bullshit on Bradford's claim that there was no conversation going on between him and Buddy. Bradford was absolutely communicating and he was doing it with a clarity that Buddy respected. She wondered what Bradford's response would have been had her dog ignored his signals. She had no doubt Bradford could defend himself, but she couldn't imagine him ever mistreating an animal.

She'd been impressed with how he'd handled the minis he'd led to the pasture. Some were well-behaved, some were still fearful around people. Charlie, one of the newest rescues, often still panicked whenever anyone went into his stall. She'd intended to lead him out herself, but when she'd returned to get him she'd found Bradford in his stall, sitting on a clean area of shavings, allowing Charlie to sniff him from head to foot.

Some people had to be told that towering over a miniature horse often intimidated them—especially those who were struggling with trusting people. Bradford appeared to instinctively know what Charlie needed and adapted his behavior without fanfare. Joanna's heart was thudding wildly in her chest when Bradford walked by her with Charlie like it was nothing at all.

Bradford looked down at Buddy. "I'm surprised he doesn't sleep in the house. I took you for someone who would have him at the foot of your bed."

Guilty as charged. "It's his choice, not mine. Whenever a new mini comes in they have to be quarantined on the other side of the barn. Horses are herd animals and isolation can be stressful for them. Buddy stays with the newbies straight through the night. Sometimes I think he thinks he's a horse and they're his herd. If you watch him in the field today you'll see him moving them around like he's the alpha and watching for predators."

"What predators do you get around here?"

"Mostly coyotes. Once in a while we'll get a bobcat or a bear. I put all the horses away at night to be safe, but Buddy sounds the alarm if anything even thinks about coming near his herd."

Bradford smiled down at the dog. "Good boy."

Buddy's tail went wild again, but his behind stayed planted on the ground.

The sound of stone crunching beneath tires caught Joanna's attention. She checked the time on her watch. "Oh, my God, it's already ten. That'll probably be Leslie and her son, Paul, coming to help. They're staying in the hunting cottage on the other side of the pasture." At first Joanna wasn't going to share more than that, but she decided it might help Bradford connect with them. "Leslie lost Paul's father a few months ago in a motorcycle accident. They weren't married so his family swooped in and booted her and Paul out of the house that was only in Paul's name. They've lawyered up and are trying to fight it, but in the meantime they have no place to live, so they're here with me. Paul has been taking it really hard. First his father, now he feels like he's lost that side of his family as well. I do what I can for them, but Leslie is too proud to accept anything more than a place to live while she figures out her housing."

Bradford didn't say anything but he placed his pick against the wall and followed Joanna to the driveway. Introductions were made then Leslie offered to finish the stalls. There were only two left so Joanna agreed.

Paul hung back. At thirteen he was in the awkward, gangly stage. His clothing was worn, but clean. "Do you need anything done this morning?" he asked without raising his eyes from the ground.

"The barn is just about done. Everyone is fed and out. Your mom will have those two stalls done before you could even get back there. You can visit with Charlie if you'd like. He needs all the human interaction he can get."

Paul nodded and was about to walk away when Bradford said, "Wait. Paul, someone gave me something yesterday that I have no use for. Any chance you could use an extra skateboard?"

Paul's face lit up as he lifted his eyes to Bradford's. "I don't have mine here and we can't—" He stopped, a sad expression came and went then he said, "I'll take it. Thank you."

"Be right back." Bradford jogged to the house and was back in a heartbeat with not only the skateboard but a bag of snacks. "Take these as well. Joanna fed me cake for breakfast. Is she plotting to make me fat?"

Joanna laughed. "Yep, that's the plan."

Paul tucked the skateboard under one arm while inspecting the contents of the bag. "Thanks. I'll definitely eat all this."

Leslie returned and Paul showed her what Bradford had given him. "Thank you," she said. "I've been meaning to pick him up another board, now I don't have to. And boys his age are a bottomless pit when it comes to food. Did you thank him, Paul?"

"He did," Bradford replied. "And I'm glad I found a home for the board."

Paul shifted with the impatience of the young. "Mom, Joanna said Charlie needs company. Mind if I go down to the pasture?"

"Sure, honey. I'll join you in a few." Once Paul was out

of earshot, Leslie sighed. "I'm worried about him. He doesn't want to see any of his old friends."

"Should I ask Angelina to bring Whitney over again? They seemed to get along," Joanna asked.

Leslie pocketed her hands and shrugged. "Maybe? I don't know. The boys like each other but they are in very different places. Angelina is marrying a movie star, Whitney is training with professional soccer players and attending a private school—Paul and I are living week to week and careful of how much we spend on groceries each week."

"Oh, Leslie. If you need anything."

Leslie shook her head. "You've already done so much for us. I'm applying for work every day, something will come through. As soon as I have a steady income we'll be back on track." She blinked back tears. "We're grateful to be here. Things will work out." She let out a shaky breath and said, "Well, it was nice to meet you, Bradford. Sorry that this is your first impression of me. I'm usually much more upbeat."

Bradford gave her a long look. "I'm sorry about Paul's father."

Leslie hugged her arms around her waist. "Me too. I still can't believe he's gone. We were together since high school. Almost got married back then but we decided to build a house instead. Then I got pregnant. There was just never extra money to pay for a wedding. We always thought there would be more time later when we could have something nice." She wiped a tear from the corner of her eye. "Sorry, there I go again. I need to stop. Nice to meet you, Bradford. Joanna, tell me what you need as far as tonight and chores. I don't mind doing them all."

"I'll text you," Joanna said. Her heart broke for Leslie, but she held her sympathy in because that wasn't what Leslie needed. Leslie had already cried for hours while Joanna sat and listened. They were entering the stage where Leslie needed to pretend she had her shit together. Joanna wanted to help her more but wasn't sure how to best do it.

After Leslie had gone to join Paul, Bradford said, "She seems like a nice enough person."

"No background check on her?"

"She has fifty-eight dollars in her savings account and six thousand dollars in credit card debt. She was in college, major undeclared, before she got pregnant and dropped out to raise her son."

The ease with which he revealed that he knew more about Leslie than even Joanna did was disconcerting. "Do you ever think it might be better to get to know people the old-fashioned way? You know, like through asking them questions as you get to know them?"

Bradford frowned. "No. Information is power."

She cocked her head to one side. "So, you always have to have the upper hand?"

He didn't answer, but the expression in his eyes was telling. It made sense that he would, but Joanna was concerned what that would mean as far as having any kind of meaningful relationship with him. One date? Two? A few hot romps? If that was all they had then his issues weren't hers.

Was that all she wanted with him, though? It was too easy to imagine waking up with him, sharing the barn chores, then falling into his kisses each night.

Aly would ask me if that's a realistic dream to indulge in. And she'd be right. I don't know what he is looking for after today. All he's said is that this is where he wants to be.

I wanted to be with him, but now that I have, what does it mean? She wasn't used to having sex outside of a steady relationship. *What do I want it to mean?*

She sighed. *I see why it's not a good idea to have sex with someone right away. I feel so close to him, but how much do I really know about him?*

She cleared her throat. "If you weren't here I'd spend the morning working with the horses and the afternoon writing. What would you like to do?"

He gave her a look that she guessed would frustrate her for as long as she knew him. There were no answers in his eyes, no hint of what he was thinking in his expression. It was likely a learned defense. His silence protected him, maintained his control in situations that made him uncomfortable.

Communication requires words with me—I'm not Buddy.

She was debating what she could say to encourage him to open up, when another vehicle pulled up her driveway. This one was a truck with a horse trailer in tow. "Oh, no."

"Who is it?" Bradford asked as he spun on his heel to face the approaching truck, standing taller as he did as if in preparation for battle.

"It's my parents." Joanna waved at the couple climbing out of the truck.

She glanced at Bradford. His expression remained carefully blank. She took his hand and gave it a reassuring squeeze. His hand tightened around hers painfully, the only tell that he was uncomfortable. Tapping the back of his hand lightly, she called attention to something she was reasonably certain he wasn't aware of. "Easy there, I need these fingers for chores later."

His grip immediately loosened. "Why are your parents here?"

"I don't know, but I have a feeling they're about to tell us."

BRADFORD WAS FREAKING the fuck out on the inside, but he'd learned early how to keep his feeling about anything to himself. Her parents? Were they there to meet him? Would they ask him questions he had no idea how to answer?

They wouldn't want the truth. *I had the best night—and morning—fucking your daughter. What are my plans? I have no idea.*

What am I doing with her if I don't know where my head is yet? I don't know. I've tried and failed to stay away from her.

What do I do for a living? You don't want to know.

Joanna's mother was a beautiful, albeit older, duplicate of her. They shared so many features they looked more like sisters than mother and daughter. She was dressed in jeans and a T-shirt that looked straight out of Joanna's closet. Her father was a tall man, easily Bradford's height, with a leaner physique, a mop of gray hair, and an easy smile.

Her mother came to a stop about a foot from where he and Joanna stood. She glanced down at their linked hands then shot a look at her daughter before continuing. "I'm Lydia, Joanna's mother."

Buddy bounded up to Lydia and jumped up on her, knocking her a little off her feet. She righted herself then bent to pat Buddy's head. The dog was about to jump on Joanna's father as well when Bradford said, "Buddy, sit." Buddy looked from Joanna to Bradford then sat, wagging his tail with his tongue hanging out. He was a goofy dog, but easy enough to like. Bradford released Joanna's hand. "Bradford."

She stepped forward to hug her mother. "Mom, you didn't tell me you were coming by."

"And you didn't mention you'd have company," her mother murmured in a low tone that Bradford likely wasn't meant to hear, but he did.

Joanna's father shook Bradford's hand. "My name's Gerry. I've heard your name before."

Joanna greeted him with a hug as well. "He's Ian's friend."

"So, did you drive in early this morning to meet the horses?" Joanna's mother asked Bradford.

"Mom." Joanna said her mother's name in reprimand.

Bradford wasn't about to lie, but not every truth needed to be proclaimed either. "It's my first time here. I have to say I'm impressed with the facility as well as its goal."

Joanna's father beamed at that. "We're proud of what Joanna has accomplished as well."

"In fact, that's why we're here," her mother said as she referenced the horse trailer behind them. "Joanna, don't be upset."

Joanna tensed beside Bradford. "What did you do?"

Her mother looked to her husband for backup. "I tried to call you, but you didn't pick up. I even sent a text this morning. No answer."

"Sorry." Joanna made a pained face while not looking her mother in the eye. "I was busy."

"We'd keep him at our place," her father said, "but our stalls are full right now. He's no trouble and we'll help you find a home for him. With all the trainers you have coming in and out of here, we figured he'd have a better chance of getting what he needs here."

From where he was standing Bradford looked at the trailer. A white nose was poking out of a side window on the trailer but it didn't look small enough to belong to a mini.

"He's not as old as he looks," Joanna's mother interjected. "Put some weight on him and he'll be gorgeous."

Joanna moved over a foot or so until she also saw the large white nose. "You know I don't train full-size horses. I'm also really careful about how many I take on." She looked up at Bradford. "Rescues go under all the time and the number one reason is they overextend." Even while she shook her head, she said, "I do know a couple of rescues that might have room for him, though."

If she was looking for Bradford's support, she had it. Although this was the first animal rescue he had any personal experience with, he'd seen many close over the years for taking on more than they could manage.

"Meet him first, then decide what to do with him." Her

father began to walk toward the back of the trailer. "Lydia, tell them how he rescued himself."

"We took our stock trailer to the auction last night because Teri, you know our neighbor's daughter? She has a farm near the store that used to be Tommy's Convenience."

Joanna linked her hand with Bradford's again. Just above a whisper she said, "I know I sound cold, but my parents would bring me a new rescue every week if I let them. They are not the kind of people who should go to animal auctions because they always come home with something. The town issued them a warning about how many animals they're allowed on their property. They can't start bringing them all here."

"That makes sense," Bradford said. He didn't want to get in the middle of their squabble, but he understood the line Joanna was attempting to hold.

Her mother continued, "Anyway, Teri is starting to raise alpaca and we'd heard there were several coming through the auction. Sometimes things work out that way—the perfect find happens just when someone needs it most."

"That's not an alpaca," Joanna said after stretching to look at the side of the trailer again.

"No, it's an Appaloosa. No name. No papers. Wait until you see him, it'll break your heart. Not only was he abused, but he was also starved. The poor thing is completely blind."

"You're killing me, Mom." Joanna brought a hand to her mouth. "He can stay, but just until we find a better placement for him."

Her mother looked toward Bradford. "You would never

know he's blind. He's not nervous at all. This is one smart horse. We were loading the alpaca onto our trailer and he unlatched his gate and filed right onto the trailer with them."

"What?" Joanna asked.

Waving her hands in the air for emphasis, her mother said, "I'd never seen anything like it. It was as if he knew nothing good would happen to him if he stayed where he was and decided to take a chance on us. He stood there in the middle of the alpaca like he belonged with them and when we tried to get him off the trailer he refused to budge. I sent your father in to pay for him which, by the way, was more than he went for because a meat buyer had already purchased him and we had to bribe him to get him to give him up. I don't know why, there's hardly any meat on him."

Her father unlatched the back of the trailer and called out after lowering the ramp. "He might have been headed off to a zoo. They pay by carcass rather than weight."

Joanna's hand shook in Bradford's before they both sprinted toward the back of the trailer as soon as the horse came into view.

Head hung low, the horse wobbled off the trailer on the thinnest legs Bradford had ever seen on a horse. Every one of the animal's ribs protruded, his hips looked like wings behind him and his face was gaunt. One of his eyes was missing, the other cloudy. There were marks on his chest and shoulder—marks that looked as if they'd been inflicted by a whip. The spot just above the horse's hooves was bald and raw from likely being cobbled for long periods of time. Bradford's stomach churned with anger at whoever had mistreated this creature. He stepped forward and laid a hand on the horse's thin neck.

The horse raised his head. The world narrowed, and for a moment there was only Bradford and the pain the horse had endured. Then the horse knickered and leaned into his touch. Bradford blinked back his welling emotion. This animal had gone through hell only to be tossed away as if it were trash and somehow it still craved a kind hand.

"No one will ever hurt you again," Bradford muttered. "I'll make sure of that."

Joanna placed her hand next to Bradford's on the horse's neck. "He might not make it, Bradford. Sometimes they don't when they're this neglected, but I'll call the vet to come out and we'll do our best."

Bradford couldn't look her in the eye—she would have seen too much of his own pain if he had. He cleared his throat. "I'll cover his expenses. Consider it a donation to your rescue. Tell me what he needs and he'll have it."

Joanna wrapped her arms around his waist and hugged him. "Well, okay. I guess I also rescue full-size horses."

Chapter Thirteen

AFTER SETTLING THE rescue horse into a stall in the quarantine area of the barn and putting in an emergency call to the vet, Joanna was alone in the aisle with her mother. "I couldn't have left him there either, Mom."

"We didn't choose him," her mother said, "he chose us. I should have taken a photo of him trying to hide between the alpaca. He knew we were his only chance, and I couldn't take that from him."

Joanna watched the horse move restlessly around the large stall. He had water, but food would wait for the okay from the vet. A special diet would have to be introduced slowly. "Do you think he'll make it?"

"The will to live is a powerful thing. When I saw him, I pictured you writing him into a series of books one day. It wasn't this horse's time to die and he knew it. I have to believe he came into our lives for a reason."

"I'll do what I can for him, Mom. If he's suffering too much, I'll do what I have to as well. Sometimes the kindest thing to do is the hardest."

Her mother nodded. "I know. I have a good feeling

about him though. He belongs here with you."

Joanna remembered how Bradford had connected to the horse as soon as it had stepped off the trailer. It was as if Bradford had met a survivor of a journey he'd been on himself. *Please, God, don't let this horse die. Please help me save it—and Bradford.*

Pulling her back to the present, her mother said, "So, when were you going to tell us you and Bradford are dating?"

"It just happened." *And I don't know if we are dating. He could leave today with no plans of coming back.* "And before you ask, it's too early to know any more than we make each other smile."

"That's a good beginning." Her mother held out a hand to the horse and snapped her fingers. The horse made his way over to the sound and nuzzled her hand. "I like him."

"He's very sweet, considering what he's been through."

"I was referring to Bradford."

The same applies to him. "I like him too."

"What do you know about his family?"

"Nothing I can share, but he didn't have an easy childhood."

"Sophie has only wonderful things to say about him."

"Mom, are you talking to the Barringtons about me again?"

"Mothers talk. Sophie and I have a lot in common."

"Really? What do you and one of the richest women in the country have in common?" Sure, she was giving her mother shit, but sometimes it was the only way to get the whole story out of her.

Her mother's grin was shameless. "You. We'd both like to see you happily married."

"I want that too, Mom, but one step at a time. I met a man I'm interested in seeing more of. It may or may not go anywhere." She looked around. "Speaking of Bradford, where did he go?"

"Oh, I think Dad took him outside to grill him."

BRADFORD HAD NEVER been the kind of man a woman took home to meet her parents. He didn't do idle chitchat. He wasn't a smooth talker. If walking away from Joanna's father wouldn't have hurt Joanna's feelings, Bradford would have done just that. Instead he'd listened to the older man talk sports for the last ten minutes and braced himself for the questions he was sure would come.

"Not much of a sports fan, are you?" her father asked.

"No, sir."

Her father frowned. "You can call me Gerry."

Bradford met his gaze without acknowledging that he would or wouldn't.

After a pause, her father said, "You're not my daughter's usual type."

There really wasn't anything polite a man could say to that so once again Bradford chose not to respond. Most people, unless they were harming someone and he couldn't stop them, had little ability to strike at Bradford in any way that hurt.

The smile her father gave Bradford surprised him. "That's a good thing. Joanna has always been strong-willed and I applaud that, but if she's with someone who isn't the same she quickly loses respect for them. She dated this one man, I forget his name, but he really liked her—enough that he took her home to meet his family. When she found out he let his grandmother pay him to mow her lawn, she was done with him. His head was still spinning as she tossed him out the door. She told us she couldn't be with a man who didn't mow his grandmother's lawn for free, and I had to give her that. My daughter knows what she wants and won't settle for less."

That was Bradford's impression of Joanna as well. He tried to imagine Joanna with a man like her father had described and couldn't. "The world is full of all kinds of people." It was a noncommittal response but the best he could come up with.

"It sure is." Gerry turned to face Bradford. The smile returned to Gerry's face. "I remember being in your shoes. Lydia's father took me aside when we first started dating and polished his shotgun the whole time we spoke."

Bradford chuckled at that. "That's one way to get a point across."

"It didn't stop us from running a little wild, but it did make me look over my shoulder a lot while we did."

Bradford laughed at that as well. He could see where Joanna got her sense of humor and her easygoing nature.

Gerry raised a hand. "The thing is—I know you're both adults. We're not here to judge what goes on, but we are here if you need us. Be good to our daughter, and you can call me anytime—night or day—and we'll be there for you."

His words hung there in the air, too kind for Bradford to immediately accept. Bradford texted his number to Gerry. "If you need anything, this is the best way to reach me."

Gerry looked down at the message that popped up on his phone. "How did you know my number?" He shrugged. "Must be one of those new phone to phone apps. Am I right?"

"Sure." Bradford had committed Gerry's number to memory back when he'd first looked into Joanna's life. The clarity of his memory was both a blessing and a curse. Some people called it having a photographic memory, but that wasn't a real thing. He just retained information better than most, a skill that had served him well for not leaving a paper trail of evidence.

"Looks like the women are coming to make sure I haven't scared you off," Gerry said. "Quick, look terrified of me. I need them to know I'm doing my job."

A laugh rumbled out of Bradford that put a smile on both Joanna and her mother's face. Gerry lifted and dropped one shoulder, looking pleased with himself. "That works just as well."

When Joanna rejoined them, she slid under his arm and laid her head on his chest as if they'd known each other forever and it was natural for them to do. "The vet said he'll be here in a few. Cross your fingers for good news."

"Whatever it takes," Bradford said firmly.

The smile she sent his way was strained. "Whatever *is best* for him. Sometimes, Bradford, things are not within our control."

Bradford didn't like that answer, but he did like the prognosis the vet gave the horse after doing a full examination. There was a feeding schedule to be strictly adhered to and shots that were needed but could wait until the horse was stronger.

Volunteers and trainers dropped by the barn to meet the new horse. The quality of the people Joanna surrounded herself with said a lot about who she was. The horse would find nothing but kindness at their hands.

As soon as the vet left, Joanna's parents announced they would need to be going as well. Joanna's mother hugged her then took Bradford by surprise by hugging him as well. The expression on his face must have revealed his discomfort because Gerry was laughing as he shook Bradford's hand afterward. "Remember what I said, son," Gerry said as he closed his wife's door, walked around and climbed into the driver's seat of his truck, and pulled out.

"What did he say?" Joanna asked.

There was no reason to lie. "He told me I could call him if there was ever anything I needed."

Joanna snuggled against Bradford's chest. "He likes you."

Bradford kissed Joanna's forehead. "That's good because I like his daughter."

After a pause, Joanna said, "I was thinking."

"Uh oh."

"You probably have to get back to your place tonight. I'm sure you have a ton of work waiting for you."

"Not as much as you'd think." She was right, he did need to leave. Their second date didn't end with him moving in. He shook his head, freaked a little that such a thought was even bouncing around in his head.

"How far away do you live?"

Locally? "Less than an hour."

"I have an idea. It might be a crazy one or it might be a wonderful one. Really, whatever you decide is okay."

He held her back. "What are you hatching in that beautiful head of yours?"

She bit her bottom lip, looked away, looked up at him again. *Whatever she wanted he doubted he could deny her.* "You seemed to really connect with the rescue my parents brought today. I'll need help with him. What do you think of coming by a little every day and working with him?"

What is she asking me? He studied her face. "You want to hire me?"

"Oh, no. I wouldn't be paying you." She blushed. "I'd just like to see you."

"Daily?" He liked the idea of that more than he was comfortable admitting.

She wrinkled her nose. "It doesn't have to be anything formal. Come by when you can, spend some time with him, walk him around. If you want to hang out we can spend some time together. If not—"

He looped his arms around her hips and turned her so she was flush against the front of him. "What do *you* want?"

She met his gaze and the emotion burning there was so intense it set his own heart racing crazily. "I'd like to spend time with you. How much? I don't know yet, but I don't want you to leave today and not come back."

He tucked her beneath his chin, held her close, and breathed the moment in. He'd given up trying to make sense of his strong attachment to her. "I don't want that either."

"I don't dive into relationships as fast as we have. It's kind of wonderful and kind of scary all at once."

He adjusted their position so he could see her face. "I could not describe what we're doing better than that."

She let out an audible breath. "So, go home tonight and come back tomorrow. If it feels right, come back the next day." She searched his face. "Or stay over if that's where the day takes us, but I need a little time to breathe tonight and find my footing again."

He kissed her gently then. Everything she was saying rang true and matched his own needs. He wanted to be with her, but he also needed a little space to get his shit together.

"What time do you want me back tomorrow?"

"Depends on what you'd like to help with. Chores start at eight a.m."

"What time do you shower?" he asked with a grin he couldn't hold back.

Her cheeks flushed and she looked up at him with a flutter of lashes. "Seven."

"Want company?"

She ran her hands up his chest and linked them behind his neck. "Better get here at six then. I don't like to rush."

The kiss that followed was a mix of shared laughter and desire. He didn't want to leave her, but time away would make returning that much sweeter. After breaking off the kiss, he helped her clean up a little, then grabbed his bag and waved to her as he drove off.

He was still smiling as he let himself into his apartment nearly an hour later. Still smiling as he fell asleep that night. Definitely smiling as he sped back to her place the next morning. He hadn't done a lot of thinking, just a whole lot of anticipating.

And it was good.

Chapter Fourteen

TWO WEEKS LATER Joanna finished writing a chapter book about Buddy and his journey from failure to miniature horse herd-guardian. She hoped it would inspire children who read it to see failing in one area wasn't a sign of being a failure. Buddy might not have made it as a traditional service dog, but he was still helping the cause—just in his own way.

After sending the manuscript off to her editor, Joanna stood, stretched, and headed outside to see what Bradford was up to. She had a pretty good idea where to find him.

She found him in the horse paddock he'd fenced for the rescue horse her parents had brought to the farm. Bradford was on a tractor back blading an area. He cut the engine when he noticed Joanna approaching and hopped down.

He lifted her off her feet then slid her down the front of him and kissed her deeply. She wound her arms around his neck and savored having a man in her life who knew how to properly greet his woman. She'd had two weeks of early morning sex, late night sex, time working with him on her farm, lots of laughter, and nights cuddled to his side. Joanna had never been happier.

The first night apart had been a good idea, but it had also convinced Joanna that having Bradford's toothbrush next to hers wasn't such a scary idea. He technically wasn't living with her, all he had at her place was one black bag, but he was at the farm most of each day and every night.

It could easily have felt like too much, but they were both independent by nature. Joanna returned to her schedule of working with horses in the morning and writing each afternoon. During the day Bradford spent more time with the farm's staff and volunteers than with Joanna. They adored him. He fixed fencing, painted areas, watched training sessions, cleaned stalls, and hand-walked the Appaloosa he had so far refused to name. The more time he spent on the farm, the harder it was to remember what it had been like before him.

Between kisses, Joanna asked, "What are you working on?"

He raised his head and nodded toward the run-in shed he'd built. "I brought the Appy out here yesterday to let him get some exercise and he didn't leave my side. I walked him around to show him where the fencing was and that seemed to reassure him, but last night I thought of something that would really help him—pea stone paths."

Joanna looked around and had to fight back happy tears. Bradford had made a path from the gate to the shelter for the blind horse. At the shelter he made short paths to the water trough and hay. "This is incredible."

He beamed with pride beneath her praise. "I used a different stone, less comfortable to walk on, to create a two-foot buffer before the fence so the horse has a warning that he's approaching fencing. Now I just have to show him what it all means."

"I love you." The words were out of her mouth before she considered how they might be received.

Bradford tensed and stepped back.

"It's how I feel, but you don't have to say it back, Bradford." Joanna took a deep breath. If life had a rewind button she would have used it then and not taken him by surprise like that. Like the Appaloosa he was working with, Bradford did best with slow and easy. "I'm happy with things the way they are between us."

The frown on Bradford's face would have saddened Joanna in the beginning. She would have seen it as a sign he didn't feel the same toward her, but that's not what she believed. Actions meant more to Joanna than words ever would.

The day after Bradford met Leslie and heard about her situation, a lawyer called and offered to get her back into her house—pro bono. Job offers had poured in and she accepted one that included a scholarship for her to continue her education and her son to attend a private school in the area. There was no doubt in Joanna's mind that Bradford had arranged all of that.

When her parents called and said they'd been contacted by several rescues who offered to partner with them to rehome animals, Joanna understood that Bradford was more comfortable showing her how much he cared rather than talking about it. So, no, it didn't matter if Bradford wasn't comfortable saying he loved her. In every other way that mattered he'd already shown her how he felt.

To break the tension, Joanna said, "Snowy Butt."

"What?"

"That's what we should name your Appaloosa. He's all white except for the blanket on his butt. It'd be a cute name."

Bradford didn't deny the ownership part, but he did say, "I'll run the name Snowy by him."

Joanna placed a hand over Bradford's heart. "You do that. He's past the danger zone now. It's safe to say he's staying. He should have a name."

Bradford covered her hand with his. "Snowy, huh?"

She shrugged. "Unless you have a better one for him."

He shook his head. "No, it suits him. Plus, kids would like it. Leslie said he has the right personality for a therapy horse. He likes people and not too much seems to bother him. I like the idea of him finding a purpose."

Joanna searched his face. He wasn't just talking about the future of the horse. Bradford was seeking his own purpose. Her gut clenched. *I have to be prepared for the possibility that it might not be here with me.*

Rescuing animals had taught Joanna a deeper understanding of love. It couldn't be selfish and still be healthy. She loved each and every creature that touched her life, but sometimes loving them involved letting them go when they were ready.

Bradford had gone two weeks without a nightmare. He

said that was a record. She saw it as a sign that being on her farm, being with her, was bringing him a certain amount of peace. She prayed that it was also a sign of some healing.

A whole side of Bradford was dying in order to be on Joanna's farm with her. How long would the simple life be enough for him?

How would she handle being with him if it involved him flying off to all corners of the planet and possibly not returning to her?

Things had been going so well she didn't want to bring up another topic that was sure to make him uncomfortable. There was no avoiding it, however. "I got a phone call this afternoon from Angelina."

He looked down at her with that impossible to read expression of his. "Yes?"

"They're headed off to Iceland tomorrow morning and wanted to know if you'd changed your mind."

His eyes narrowed. "I haven't."

"I was planning to go even if you didn't." She wished he would show how he felt about that possibility, but— nothing. "I've never seen Iceland or a film being made. Plus, Dylan is really excited for all of us to be there."

"You should go."

"I might. I really want to." Joanna folded her arms across her chest. "What would you say if I told you I don't want to go without you?"

He held her gaze without blinking. "I have things I'm working on here."

Her stance softened. "Snowy? We don't have to go for

long. Just a few days. You know he'd be well taken care of here."

"I said no."

Joanna gasped when he turned and walked away from her, straight out of the paddock and to his car. *Well, that went well.*

BRADFORD WASN'T DRIVING with a destination, he just needed to put some distance between himself and Joanna long enough to work through the tsunami of emotion crashing through him. He pulled off onto a dirt road and parked.

Fuck. Fuck. Fuck.

He called the one person who knew him almost better than he knew himself. When he answered, Bradford barked, "Ian, listen, don't speak."

"Okay," Ian said in an urgent tone that meant he probably assumed Bradford was being held somewhere at gunpoint.

Bradford took a deep breath and blurted, "Joanna said she loves me."

"That's what this is about?" Ian laughed, then coughed, then shut up.

Slamming his hands on his steering wheel, Bradford growled, "She makes me happy. Me. Happy. Like I am fucking smiling when I wake up in the morning and I can sleep like a regular person. The past two weeks have been fucking heaven. I haven't watched the news, and I have no idea if the rest of the world still exists. If there's shit going on anywhere, I don't even know that I care. Being with her is that fucking good."

"Okay."

"I've met the farm's veterinarian three times and I don't even know his fucking last name. He said it. I didn't hear him. I don't care. I don't even swear at the farm."

"Wow."

"I own a horse now. Or maybe I don't. I don't fucking know. I have goals for him and enjoy working with him. The more time I spend with Joanna, the more time I want to. The people at her farm are beginning to feel like—*friends*. Have I fucking lost my mind?"

"Is that a rhetorical question or am I allowed to answer?"

"I'm serious, Ian. I might be having a complete breakdown. If I am, I know too much for you to let me live. You need to fucking take me out if I get any worse."

Ian chuckled. "I'm not taking you out because you fell in love."

Bradford closed his eyes. "I thought love was supposed to feel good."

"Uh," Ian said, "it's more complicated than that. It's scary as hell to realize you care about someone else more than you care about yourself. What did you say when she told you she loved you?"

"Nothing."

"That's not the ideal response."

"I know." He rubbed his hands over his face. "That wasn't even the worst part."

"No?"

"She wants me to go to Iceland with everyone tomorrow."

"I've heard about that trip. You should go. Dylan was disappointed that you declined."

"Outside of the fact that I can only be around Clay for about ten seconds before I want to punch him in the head, my gut tells me it's a bad idea. My gut is never wrong."

"You don't have to worry about Clay. When I heard he outed your address to the meatheads I took him aside and woke him up to a few harsh realities. One being what I'd do to him if he got you killed."

Bradford sighed and conceded, "That was actually nice of you. Thanks."

"I'm not sure what to make of this softer side of you. Remember when the Thing turned back into a man in the *Fantastic Four?* This is like that. I'm happy for you, but could I kick your ass now?"

"Thanks for being absolutely no help, Ian." Bradford prepared to end the call.

"Wait. Sorry. Listen, Joanna is a wonderful woman. I've known you a long time and I've never seen you happy. If you feel for her half as much as I love Claire, it's worth riding out the part where you feel out of control and wrong all the time. If you make it past that—there's so much good stuff."

"I already said no to Iceland." *And walked away. She's probably furious.*

"So, change your mind. You don't have to fly over with Clay and everyone else. Get a private plane. Meet them there. I'm going to throw out this wild concept—

compromise. That heaven you describe cannot be sustained without a whole lot of compromising. It's worth it though. I'm proud of you, Bradford. Look at you—all grown up and not killing anyone."

"Shut the fuck up."

"Tell her how you feel then take her to Iceland. You've had a lot of shitty things happen to you. Let yourself have this."

Images of Joanna looking up at him with unfiltered love in her eyes filled his thoughts. She didn't hold back. When things got tough she didn't sprint for her car and drive off. She deserved to be with a man who had the balls to stick around and tell her how he felt.

He put his car in drive, pulled out onto the road, and turned around. "Thanks, Ian. I know what I need to do now."

Ian said, "Before I forget, there's something I wanted to ask about Daphne—"

"Whatever it is can wait, Ian. I need to do this right. Talk to you later." Bradford ended the call without waiting for Ian's response. He drove back to Joanna's farm, back to the barn where he hoped she still was. As soon as he parked, she stepped into the driveway to meet him.

He exited his car and jogged over to about a foot from her. "Joanna."

Her eyes were full of understanding. "It's okay. I wasn't looking at the trip from your perspective, just mine. I told Angelina I'm not going."

He took both of her hands in his and took a deep breath.

"What do you think of flying over, just you and me, and meeting them there? Clay does get under my skin, but Dylan is a good guy and—and—"

"And?" she asked breathlessly.

"And I may love you."

Her smile was both kind and amused. "May?"

He pulled her to his chest and wrapped his arms around her. "Okay, I love you, Joanna. I've never felt this way for anyone and it scares the shit out of me, but I've also never been happier. Things with you are so good they don't feel real yet. But it is real. And it's time to take what we have out into the world."

She framed his face with her hands. "If you're sure."

"I'm sure."

"Could you say it again?" she asked.

"Which part?"

"That you love me. Leave off the may part."

"I love you."

"Again?" She wrinkled her nose at him playfully.

"I love you." It got a little easier each time he said it.

"Could you say it naked?"

He swept her off her feet, tossed her over his shoulder, and carried her toward the house. "I could definitely say it naked. More than once. Probably for hours."

Chapter Fifteen

J OANNA HAD NEVER been on a private plane. There were definitely perks to it. No lines. No crying children. A male attendant was there to make sure they had everything they needed at all times. Nice. Not necessary. Joanna had flown many times with much less luxury and still enjoyed herself, still it was fun to be catered to.

Going away with Bradford right after he admitted he loved her felt monumental. On one hand it was romantic like some fairy-tale honeymoon. On the other hand, Joanna worried that it was another huge leap forward, one he might not be ready for.

They'd been a couple on her farm, but she'd avoided mixing him with Aly and Angelina because she didn't want anything negative to mar what they had. *That's not healthy. If this is love and we really are moving forward together, then our friends have to be included.*

Aly is concerned because she doesn't know Bradford, but once she sees how happy I am with him she'll change her mind about him. Angelina is used to seeing me break it off with men—she needs to see us together as well. This is the real deal.

I found my forever.

Joanna fell asleep with her head on Bradford's shoulder and woke much later to the attendant speaking to Bradford. Whatever he'd said, Bradford didn't look happy about it. "I didn't request a change."

Joanna sat up and stretched. "What's wrong?"

"We're being diverted to the island Clay's friend owns. If Clay is messing with me already—"

"Relax. I'm sure there was just a change of plans. Maybe the group decided to go to the island first."

Bradford sighed. "Possibly. I don't like surprises though." He took out his phone. "I'm not getting a signal."

Joanna took out her phone. "Me either, but isn't that normal while we're in flight?"

"I have a satellite phone."

"Oh."

The attendant didn't look concerned. "The local phone service carriers have been battling it out for this area. New towers are always going up. There's been talk of jamming each other's service bands illegally. It's a problem."

"Sounds like a big one." Bradford put his phone down and went to stand. "I'll have the pilot radio a call in for me."

"We're just about to land, sir. I was asked to make sure your seat belts were secure."

Joanna said, "I'm sure everything is fine, Bradford. We'll know what's going on as soon as we land."

"We'd better." Bradford secured his belt.

From the plane window, Joanna appreciated the layout of the island that still functioned as a farm even as she prayed for a simple explanation for them changing locations. She gripped the armrests on both sides of her seat.

Bradford took her hand in his and bent to kiss her cheek. "I'm sorry. Old habits die hard. You're right, this is a fun trip. Blips are nothing more than inconveniences." He shook his shoulders. "See, I'm shaking them off."

She smiled. "Even if Clay has arranged for us to have a little private time on the island, he means well. He did kind of bring us together. It might be fun to see what he'd come up with way out here."

"I hate to give him credit for us." Shaking his head, Bradford said, "You're right, though. He did impress me with that tent. I suppose there's nothing wrong with going along with whatever this is about."

"Another adventure. You and me." She kissed him.

The kiss heated up, but was cut short when the plane bounced as it touched down. "Either way, looks like we're visiting the island first."

"It'll be fun."

He kissed the palm of her hand. "If you're here I know I'll have a good time." After the plane came to a stop they both unbuckled and gathered their things.

The caretaker of the island met them at the bottom of the plane's steps and introduced himself as Egill. He was an older man with a short beard, a thick sweater, and a black knit cap. "Right on time. **Góðan daginn.** Excuse the rush, but I did not expect you tonight so there are things I need to ready. Come. Come. I will take you to the main house."

Bradford helped the man load their luggage into the back

of his small SUV. "Does the house have a phone I could use?"

"Of course. Come, I take you there now."

Joanna was securing her seat belt when she heard Bradford swear. "What is it?"

He climbed in next to her. "I thought the plane was taxiing to park, but it took off. I don't like that."

Joanna jokingly shook her fist in the air and called out, "Clay Landon, you'll pay for this. Fool me once—"

Bradford silenced her with a kiss. "You're right. I can relax and enjoy myself as much as anyone else can." He opened his window and breathed in the cool, fresh air. "We should have plenty of light. Maybe we can go for a walk. Check the place out."

"That's the spirit."

With a smile, Bradford sat back and put his arm around Joanna. The island was large enough to have several buildings and a few pastures, but it didn't take long to cross. They were soon at the house.

Joanna spotted horses, grabbed Bradford's arm, and exclaimed, "Oh, look, they have Icelandics. Maybe we could go for a ride tomorrow."

"Yes," the caretaker said, "of course you can. I will get them ready for you in the morning. No problem. First, I will show you your room. If you are hungry there is food, although I did not have the cook come today because I thought you would be here next week. But it's okay. I'll make it work."

"Clay's slipping with his planning," Bradford said.

Joanna snuggled to his side. "Maybe he thinks by now all you need is me."

"And he'd be right." His smile told her his mood was coming back around.

The house was bright yellow with white trim and lace curtains. Joanna was glad it wasn't a mansion. The white picket fence flanking the house made it feel like they were traveling back in time to some 1950s sitcom neighborhood.

As they approached the house Joanna realized it was bigger than she'd thought. Additions had been built that matched and didn't at the same time. Set back were a few buildings that looked like they might house animals and some kind of garage. Across a wide expanse of lawn there was a dock and a boat pulled up onto the grass.

When they parked, Bradford got out to help the caretaker carry their luggage in. Joanna gathered their coats and her purse then followed them into the house. The home was surprisingly modern—almost disappointing to see. Clay's friend probably updated it without realizing how much of its charm would be lost. It was a beautiful home that felt a little like a hotel on the inside.

They followed Egill up a staircase. He said, "Use these stairs to come and go. On the other side of the hallway you will find stairs down to the kitchen. Use those if you get hungry. I'll warm some soup for you."

"Thank you," Bradford said as he placed their luggage inside the door of the bedroom Egill told them was theirs. It was beautiful, but also updated to hotel level and a little out of place.

Egill pointed to the phone beside the bed. "If you need anything, dial zero zero and it rings me. Otherwise, settle in and come down to the kitchen when you are hungry. Night is very short here if you don't close your curtains. The sun will set around midnight and come up again around three a.m."

"Three a.m." Bradford repeated the time. "We'll close the curtains. I'm doing my best not to get up that early anymore."

Joanna slipped under Bradford's arm and hugged his side. "The good news is it's light for so long. We'll definitely have time to explore. After all that sitting I can't wait to get outside. I need to freshen up first though."

"You do that. I'd join you, but I want to contact the others to see if the plan is for them to meet us here or how long Clay thinks we need to enjoy this place solo." He gave her a quick kiss before Joanna grabbed one of her bags and headed into the bathroom.

After closing the door she turned and leaned back against it. Bradford didn't like the unexpected. It made sense that he wouldn't. She wished she knew how to reassure him, but maybe only time could do that.

She met her eyes in the mirror above the sink and told herself to be patient. There were men with less issues, but they didn't make her feel the way he did. For the first time in her life she understood how it was possible to spend a lifetime with one person.

She remembered what he said about Snowy when he first met him: "Whatever it takes." Bradford was direct like that and she was learning that trait from him. She used to worry more about what people thought of her and kept her opinion more to herself.

Poor Bradford, I was a lot fucking sweeter before I met him.

Joanna smiled briefly at her own joke. She pushed off the door, hunted her toothbrush out of her bag, and assessed the damage the long flight had inflicted on her makeup. *Not as bad as I thought. A few touch-ups and I'll be ready to go.*

BRADFORD SAT ON the corner of the bed and reached into the breast pocket of his jacket for his phone. It wasn't there. He checked his other pockets—it wasn't in any of them either. He groaned as he remembered placing it on a seat on the plane when he'd considered using the pilot's radio to make a call. *And I fucking left it there.*

Careless in a way he never was.

He turned to the phone beside the bed. *Fine, I'll use that.* He picked up the receiver and hit the call button. It lit up, but there was no dial tone. He followed the wire to the wall. Everything looked fine.

Figures.

Joanna was still in the bathroom. He could probably locate Egill and use his phone before she even noticed he was gone. If the soup was ready he could return with a tray for her. He headed out of the room, going down the hallway the opposite way to the stairway Egill had said led to the kitchen.

The kitchen was empty—no sign that he'd started warming soup. Strange. The hair on the back of Bradford's neck rose. He told himself it was likely nothing, but too many things were happening that shouldn't.

He took his gun out and made his way through the kitchen. The side door was open. There were two indentations in the grass. If he were anywhere else he would say someone had just been dragged that way, but he was trying to tone down his paranoia. There was no place for it in the life he was building with Joanna.

More likely, there is a less dramatic explanation for the drag marks. Maybe Egill took out a garbage bag that had two rotten cantelopes in the bottom that dragged along the ground.

Fuck me.

Gun drawn, Bradford headed out the door and followed the trail. As soon as he turned the corner he felt the sting of a dart hitting his neck and instant drowsiness. *That's not good,* was his last thought before he face-planted in the grass.

JOANNA WAITED FOR Bradford to return; when he didn't she decided to call Egill to see if he knew where he was. No dial tone.

Clay was a romantic, but he also got involved with things to alleviate his boredom. If he was scaring Bradford and her a little in an attempt to get them to bond more, he would hear several choice words from her when she saw him again. That was exactly the kind of antic that would set Bradford off.

You went too far this time, Clay. This is not romantic and not funny.

She left the bedroom and asked herself where Bradford likely would have gone. Egill had said he would warm some soup for them. It made sense that Bradford might have started there. There was no sign of either him or Egill, but the door was open.

Joanna blamed her adrenaline rush on the stories Bradford had told her and the warnings he'd given her. There was a trail in the grass that led to the corner of the building. Heart pounding wildly in her chest, she followed it. She stopped just before the corner, took a calming breath, then bent and peered around it.

Egill was flat on his back with a gunshot to his chest. Her mouth dropped open. Her first reaction was that it had to be a sick joke. He couldn't actually be dead.

She retreated behind the corner of the house. *Fuck. Fuck. Fuck.*

Think.

Maybe he attacked Bradford and Bradford shot him.

No. That doesn't make sense. Bradford would have come to me to make sure I was safe.

Unless he didn't mean to kill him and he's afraid of going to jail so he ran.

That doesn't sound like Bradford either.

Joanna went down onto her knees and peered around the corner again. Egill was still there, still lying in a pool of his own blood, still looking dead.

Beyond Egill there were more drag marks. *Bradford. Someone has Bradford.*

Shaking from head to toe, Joanna crawled closer to Egill. His eyes were open and there was no sign of life in them. She mustered courage and turned him slightly over. *Please let him have a phone. Please.*

He did. She didn't allow herself to think that she was stealing from a dead man. All that mattered was Bradford and saving him. *Because he's still alive. He has to be.*

Please let him be.

Joanna retreated around the corner of the building on her knees then sprinted to a place behind a flowering bush. She whispered a thank you to Egill for not having his phone password protected. He had a signal. She turned off his ringer and chose to text rather than call so she wouldn't be discovered. She could only text people she knew the number for so she sent one to Angelina.

This is Joanna. I'm with Bradford on Clay's friend's island. We're in trouble. Caretaker has been murdered. Someone has Bradford. I'm hiding but I'll keep the phone with me. I don't know how many people are here with us. Contact Ian. Get help. This is not a joke. Please help us. Hurry.

The response was almost immediate. **Ian is down the hall. Hang on. I'll show him your text.**

This is Ian. I came with the group. Don't leave your hiding place. I'm on my way.

Okay.

Stay hidden. Bradford and I are trained for things like this. I'm putting men in the air as we speak. You are not alone.

Joanna swallowed her tears and fought a wave of panic. **I'm scared.**

Don't move and you'll be fine. I have a helicopter starting up now. It's going to be okay, Joanna. Stop texting and don't make a sound.

Joanna pocketed the phone and hugged her arms around herself. She'd always enjoyed haunted houses and roller coasters. She liked to consider herself a bit of a daredevil. Real fear was an entirely different animal.

Breathe. Don't move. Stay hidden and let Ian handle this.

She remembered the drag marks. Was Bradford already shot?

What if Ian gets here too late?

Bradford wouldn't let anyone hurt me. I can't sit here while someone might be hurting him.

If it gets me killed—well, at least I died doing something important.

She made her way back to where the caretaker's body was and followed the drag marks in the grass to a barn. Slowly. Carefully. Praying for calm with each step, she made her way to one of the barn's windows and crouched behind a bush there.

A loud crack echoed. A smack? Joanna held her breath, fought the temptation to look into the window, and just listened.

"Wake up. This shit is supposed to wear off fast. Wake the fuck up." It was a woman's voice and it sounded familiar, but Joanna couldn't place it. "Good. Open your fucking eyes. Look at me."

"Who are you?" Bradford asked in a slurred voice.

He's still alive. Thank God.

"You don't know my face? I thought you were the man who knew everything. You know nothing."

When Bradford didn't respond it sounded like she hit him again. "Don't you dare pass out again. Look at me. In the eye. Do you recognize these eyes?"

"No."

"They're the same as my brother—the man you killed."

"I've killed a lot of people. You'll have to be more specific." He groaned as if in response to a hit from more than her hand.

No, Bradford, don't taunt her.

Where do I know that voice from?

Joanna snuck a peek over the edge of the window. *Daphne? Claire's meek client?* She ducked back down. *She must have been stalking Bradford at the event. This is an eye for an eye.*

She's going to kill him.

In a disgusted tone, Daphne said, "Five years ago. In Quarrytown you hunted my brother down and shot him like an animal. You left him to die on the side of the road. He was twenty. Do you remember him now?"

"I do."

"Good. Because I want him to be what you think about when I kill your girlfriend in front of you. You took someone I loved. I've waited years for you to care about someone so I could take them from you. Today that's what I'll do. You'll watch your girlfriend die . . . nice and slow . . . and *then* I'll kill you."

"Your brother was a murderer. He took money from innocent people he promised to help cross the border. People trusted him and he left them to suffocate in vans just before the border. Then he disposed their bodies and went back for more. He was driving a van full of people the day I killed him. People like him don't deserve to be avenged."

"Shut up," the woman screamed. "I would kill you now but you wouldn't suffer enough."

As Daphne continued to rant, Joanna made a decision. She couldn't risk Bradford getting shot in front of her. He wouldn't hide while she was beaten, and she wouldn't be able to live with herself if he was hurt more while she hid.

She spotted what looked like a dog door and crawled toward it. Whatever Bradford was saying to Daphne had her screaming even more at him, threatening to kill him at a decibel so loud she probably would have heard it back at the house.

He's inciting her to make sure I hear them and know how dangerous she is. He does love me.

Joanna didn't look at Bradford or give him any warning for what she was about to do because the only thing she had on her side was the element of surprise. Daphne was waving her gun around wildly. Joanna decided there wouldn't be a better time.

Hunt or be hunted.

Joanna picked up a shovel, crept up behind Daphne, and hit her arm holding the gun as hard as she could. The gun went flying but the hit didn't send Daphne to the ground. She spun like a snarling fisher-cat. Her punch came fast and hard to Joanna's face.

Joanna stumbled back, angry this time. *Bitch, you think you can hit harder than a horse can kick? You have no idea.* Joanne delivered the first punch of her life with all the anger she usually bottled inside. Daphne went flying back, landing on her ass in front of Bradford.

Bradford must have broken free of whatever she had him tied with while he was arguing with her because he grabbed both of her arms and dragged them behind her while lifting her to her feet. He looked like he was still under the influence of what she'd drugged him with, but her struggles didn't free her from his hold.

Joanna scrambled to get the gun and returned with it. Her hands were shaking so much she wasn't sure what she'd hit if she tried, but there was no way she was losing the advantage they'd gained.

Bradford's face was bloody and his expression tortured. "Joanna. I've got her. You can lower the gun."

"Ian's on his way," Joanna said in a high pitch. "All we have to do is hold Daphne until then."

"Then definitely don't shoot both of us," Bradford said in a dry voice.

"You should shoot him," Daphne said. "He's a cold-blooded murderer."

"Like you?" Joanna asked, still shaking so much she was having trouble holding onto the gun. "You killed Egill."

"Do you know how many lives Bradford has taken? My brother was still a boy. He should have been given a chance to change. I could have saved him."

"He was too far gone," Bradford said.

"You don't know that," Daphne snarled. "I've watched you, Bradford. I know how easily you kill. How dare you stand in judgment of my brother. You're not God. Satan would claim you as his own. You're pure evil. How do you sleep beside that each night, Joanna? How can you bear his touch?"

"Don't let her in your head, Joanna," Bradford warned.

"Oh, aren't you able to kill in front of your girlfriend, Bradford?" The laugh Daphne let out was maniacal. "What do you plan to do with me then?"

"The law will deal with you," Bradford growled.

Daphne laughed again. "It's almost sad to see you this weak. Thank you, Joanna. I may just have a chance to do this again—if I'm lucky you'll have children and we can make a whole party of it."

Joanna stepped closer, hands shaking wildly. The stories Bradford had told her about how some people were better off dead suddenly made sense. Daphne was not only threatening them, but their future children. How much would the world really miss someone like that? "Take a step back, Bradford."

"Don't do it, Joanna," Bradford said in a low tone.

"She'll never leave us alone."

"We'll make sure she's locked up and can't hurt us."

Daphne spat in Joanna's direction. "I'm not worried. She doesn't have the guts to shoot anyone."

"You're wrong," Joanna said as a calm settled over her. Her finger hovered over the trigger. "Step back, Bradford."

"No." He brought Daphne squarely in front of himself. "Shooting her will change you, Joanna. I have her. She's not going anywhere. It would be murder and that's not who you are. It's not who I want to be. She's not worth your soul, Joanna. Don't give it to her."

As if by magic, Ian and several men appeared around them. Braford handed Daphne off to one of them and approached Joanna, who was shaking again and still holding the gun out in front of her. "Give me the gun, Joanna."

She looked down at the weapon she'd almost forgotten she still had in her hands. "Is it over?"

"It's over. We're safe." He took the gun from her, clicked the safety, and stuffed it in the back of his jeans.

Her whole body began to shake violently. "Your face is bleeding."

"So is yours." He stepped closer and cupped the side of her face Daphne had punched.

Ian signaled for his men to remove Daphne. "Joanna, I told you to hide."

Bradford wrapped his arms around Joanna and held her close. "She's hardheaded. Even her father says so."

Nothing felt real, but Bradford's teasing was a beacon luring her back from the edge of dropping to the floor and giving in to a good cry. "I saved your ass," Joanna mumbled against his chest.

He kissed the top of her head. "You did and you didn't even shoot me in the process. Remind me to get you on a range. A little gun safety never hurt anyone."

"Ungrateful jerk," Joanna joked and relaxed against Bradford, soaking in his strength. He was alive. That was all that mattered.

"How did you know?" Bradford asked Ian.

"Joanna texted Angelina. Daphne was already on my radar. There was something not right about her story for why she wanted to work with Claire. I looked into her and discovered her real name is Tina Olsen. I'm surprised you missed that."

Bradford shuddered against Joanna. "I've been a little distracted." He hugged Joanna tighter. "If anything had happened to you—"

Joanna raised her head. "I feel the same way. When I found Egill dead I thought—I was afraid that you were also—"

Bradford kissed her and it was a different kiss than they'd ever shared. This one was full of regret, love, and frustration. When he broke off the kiss, he growled. "This is my fault. I got sloppy. I usually know the background on everyone, but the night of the event all I cared about was you."

Joanna framed his face with her hands. "It was the same for me."

His smile was sad. "You are the most caring, understanding person I've ever met. I don't know what the hell you see in me, but I know I almost got you killed. That can't happen again."

A shot was fired outside, then another. Ian pressed a hand to his earpiece then nodded. "Doesn't look like you'll have to worry about Daphne/Tina anymore. She grabbed one of the men's guns, shot it, and missed them. Our sniper took her out."

"Oh, thank God," Joanna said, then froze. "Is it wrong to be glad she's dead?"

Bradford nuzzled her hair. "You're asking the wrong person."

A SHORT WHILE later, back on the mainland, Bradford

stepped out of a room filled with Joanna's friends: Dylan, Connor, Lexi and Clay. Despite how subdued Clay's greeting had been, Bradford's nerves were on edge and he couldn't summon any patience for him.

Ian followed Bradford into the hallway and out the back door of the house. "Everything has been handled with the local authorities. Egill didn't have any living family, but we arranged for him to be buried near his parents."

"Good." His head was still throbbing, partially from being drugged, possibly from the beating his head had taken, but also because he was disappointed in himself. "Joanna could have been killed today."

"But she wasn't."

Bradford spun on his friend. "Don't try to whitewash this. If she had died today it would have been for one reason and one reason alone—because she was with me."

"So, what are you going to do?"

"The only thing I can. I'll tell her it's over. I can't protect her from the shit we've done."

Ian ran a hand through his hair. "Is Claire in danger because she's with me?"

"Yes, but I've got your back."

"As I have yours." When Bradford began to say something, Ian cut him off and added, "And don't even say that's not enough because I was in that barn in less than ten minutes after I got the text. And I had a team fly over to be on standby. I was on point."

Bradford sighed. "You were, but I wasn't. There were signs that I either missed or dismissed each step of the way.

None of this would have happened had I remained focused."

"She was a sick woman with a twisted plan to hurt you. How does anyone prepare for that?"

Fisting his hands, Bradford growled, "I did leave her brother to die. I showed no mercy. What kind of man does that?"

Ian came to stand beside him. "You can't take out the trash without getting your hands dirty. We're not machines. You and I have seen too much of the ugly side of humanity. No one can fight on the front lines forever without snapping. It's time for you to give up that life, Bradford, and let someone else fight in the trenches. We've done our time there. Come work with me and we'll help people do what we did—but better. There has to be a way to get ahead of the problem. Who were Tina and her brother before they chose violence and crime? Did they struggle in poverty? What happened to their parents? What made them into who we killed? If they'd had someone like us on their side earlier could we have prevented them from making the choices they did? I don't know the answers, but that's where I want to put my energy now. You should join me."

Bradford shook his head and looked away. He understood what Ian was saying, but he couldn't shake the knowledge of how close Joanna had come to dying because of him.

Ian put a hand on his shoulder. "Imagine how different your life would have been if someone had listened and helped your sister before it was too late. That's the moment we'll try to prevent and we can do it without shooting anyone. There are foster programs that can be improved, safe houses for people trying to escape gangs, job training and placement for those who feel they have no other choices. We can't go back in time and change what we've done, but we can help others not have a need to follow in our footsteps."

"What about when that's not good enough?"

"There are people who'll step in and handle it. We've done our tour of duty. I'm carving out a real life for myself now. I'll help you do the same."

Bradford rubbed his hands over his face. "I don't know. I love her, Ian, but is that enough?"

Ian's phone rang. He checked it and smiled. "It's my mother."

Bradford shook his head.

"I have to." Ian answered then held out the phone to Bradford. "She wants to talk to you. Apparently you're not answering your phone again."

A laugh bubbled within Bradford. "Seriously?"

Ian waved the phone for Bradford to take. "She'll only call back."

Bradford took the phone and Ian stepped back inside the house. "Hi, Sophie."

"Bradford. Is everything okay? I always worry when I can't reach you."

"Sorry, I misplaced my phone." That part was true at least.

"Something's wrong. A mother always knows these things. What happened?"

"Everything's fine."

"Did you have a fight with Joanna?"

"A fight? No." His voice was tight with emotion.

"But something happened. Bradford, that girl adores you. Talk to me."

He normally wouldn't have said a word. Maybe it was the influence of the remaining drugs in his system. Or maybe it was how much he hated that he didn't see the day ending without him breaking things off with Joanna. "I'm not the man for her." Not being able to keep Joanna safe was a deal breaker for him—he'd told her so himself.

"Don't say that."

"Not saying it doesn't make it less true. You don't know the things I've done, Sophie. Unforgivable things that come with dangerous consequences. I can't change that no matter how much I wish I could."

"You listen to me, Bradford, there is no one on this planet who is perfect. You might think I can't possibly understand, but I do. I know what it's like to feel like I've let people down. I spent years doubting myself, hating myself. Danger? Yes, I brought that to my family as well. Ask Ian about my sister. He'll tell you."

Bradford didn't need to. He'd watched the Patrice drama unfold through Ian's eyes. She was the one who paid someone to kidnap one of the youngest Barringtons right out of the hospital nursery. Ian had told Bradford about the pain that had brought Sophie as well as the rest of the family. Patrice had tried but failed to kill Sophie's child, ruined Dale's political career, and anyone who'd stood in her way had met an untimely death. So, yes, Sophie understood how

Bradford felt to a certain degree. "I appreciate what you're saying, Sophie, but Joanna needs someone with a lot less baggage than I come with."

"Joanna needs a man who loves her. That's it. Do you?"

Bradford swallowed hard. "I do."

"Then stick it out. Love wins against hate every single time if we stay faithful to it. Dale never left me. No matter what my sister did to our family, no matter how much I fell apart—he stayed. We both made mistakes, but we didn't give up on each other. If you really love Joanna, love her enough to stay. That's the kind of man she deserves . . . one who sticks out the bad times long enough for the good times to come back around."

With his heart beating wildly in his chest, Bradford turned and looked back at the house. He'd always been good at leaving. He'd been about to do it again, but he was being given a choice again.

He could walk away and watch from a distance as Joanna moved on and started a life with another man or he could . . . stay. "Thank you, Sophie." He thought of the way she'd always included him, continued to invite him to her home although he always declined, called even when he didn't answer her. "For not giving up on me . . . and for everything."

"You've been a good friend to Ian. I don't know, and I'm sure I don't want to know, the trouble the two of you have gotten yourselves into over the years, but he told me you saved his life more than once. He considers you his brother and that makes you family. We love you, Bradford."

"I—I—"

"I know. Now, tell me about Joanna."

"We've had a rough day. Regardless of what I decide, I wouldn't blame her if she calls it quits after today. I put her through hell."

"Are you in Iceland with Clay?"

Bradford groaned. "Yes."

"Sometimes the best way to move on from a bad situation is to do something good for someone else."

"What are you suggesting?"

"Clay feels like he failed with you and Joanna. He thinks you hate him."

"Hate? No."

"He might seem like someone who has everything, but he was raised by people who only wanted the money they thought they could steal from him. Lexi told me he never really had a home growing up; he was always at boarding schools. He never learned how to connect with people. This fairy godfather thing is his way of trying to get close to people."

"I don't need Clay's help."

"But he needs yours. If you're looking for a way to put a smile back on Joanna's face—ask Clay for magical assistance. All he's looking for is acceptance."

Bradford was trying to be a better person, but could he be that nice? He remembered the tent and all the work that had gone into planning it. Clay was confrontational, often condescending and a pain in the ass even on his best day—but he certainly knew how to wow Joanna. After what

Bradford had put her through, he was willing to agree to almost anything to make her smile again. "I'll talk to him."

"You won't regret it."

"Sophie, can you see someone like me married with kids?"

When she answered her voice was thick. "Yes, but the real question is can you picture your children calling someone like me Grandma?"

Bradford chuckled as his heart opened and finally let those possibilities in. "As long as you're okay that they might swear like sailors."

She laughed. "Have you met my sons? Besides, I hear you have a swear jar now."

"How—?"

"Lydia tells me everything. I can't wait to meet Snowy. Promise to invite us out soon."

"I will. Thanks again, Sophie."

Bradford was on his way back to the group when Clay stepped into the hallway. They both froze. "Clay, I need to talk to you about something."

Lips pressed together, looking like a boy being called into the principal's office, Clay made his way over to Bradford. "You don't have to say it," Clay said. "Ian laid into me about how I had exposed you when I shouldn't have. I've hung my magic wand up for good."

"What happened wasn't your fault. There was no way you could have known she would divert my plane to the island." After letting out a long breath, Bradford said, "Besides, I need your help."

Clay's face lit up. "You do?" Then his expression turned skeptical. "Is this a joke?"

Good comes from good? Here goes. "I've decided to propose to Joanna but I don't want to do it here. And I want to do it in a way that is so wonderful she forgets all about what she saw back on that island. Will you help me come up with something that good?"

Clay was all smiles. "That's why my card says extraordinaire."

Bradford flexed his shoulders. *You'd better be right, Sophie.*

Chapter Sixteen

A FEW WEEKS later Joanna paused her work with a rescue mini to watch Bradford with Snowy. He had taught the horse to navigate his pasture on the stone paths and had moved on to verbal commands. When Snowy was grazing on grass and Bradford called him he did a kind of shuffle around until he found the pea stone. Then he'd run toward Bradford. The problem they were encountering was Snowy needed to stop before crashing into him. Patience, consistency, and compassion were paying off though. That morning Bradford called Snowy, spoke as he ran to him, then gave him a firm command to whoa. The horse stopped a few feet from Bradford and waited for Bradford to come to him.

The trip to Iceland, especially the start of it, still felt surreal. She and Bradford had stayed on with the group afterward and vacationed as if nothing had happened. They'd watched Dylan finish his filming, enjoyed touring glaciers and hot springs, and had a good amount of phenomenal sex. It was almost as if they hadn't nearly both been killed.

Joanna would have pushed Bradford to talk about it, but

he was showing her how seriously he'd taken the experience. When they returned back to the States, Bradford accepted a job offer to work with Ian. They had offices in Boston, New York, and Washington, but Bradford said most of his work could be done with a laptop and phone. When he explained the projects he was working on with Ian, Joanna understood he was making changes to his lifestyle so they could have a future. He didn't need to say it when he was doing it.

Bradford had set up a security system at Joanna's farm. Before Iceland she would have said it wasn't necessary, but she understood his need for caution. She slept better knowing the extra precautions were there.

For a man who'd seemed reluctant at first to spend any time at all with her family, Bradford had warmed up to the idea of having her parents drop in often. He and her father had even gone fishing twice together. Once on a huge yacht with Connor and once at the pond on her parents' farm. They all seemed to have equally enjoyed both.

A car pulled into the driveway and parked near the barn. Joanna waved to her parents and breathed a sigh of relief that they didn't have a trailer in tow.

Another car parked beside them with Angelina, Connor, Whitney, and Dylan inside.

Aly pulled in beside them.

Joanna's mouth dropped open when more and more cars pulled in and filled the field beside the barn. Sophie. Dale. All the Barrington children, their spouses and their children.

Mrs. Tellier? What's going on?

One of the trainers came by and took the lead line and

pony from Joanna. That was when Joanna realized all of her staff was circling around as well. Even Leslie was there with her son.

Just when she was about to walk over and ask Bradford what this was about, she heard bells ringing. Six white ponies were pulling a white wire-and-glass Cinderella pumpkin carriage. It stopped beside Joanna. A man in a white tux stepped down and unrolled a piece of paper. "Joanna Ervin?"

"Yes."

"You are hereby invited to spend the rest of your life with a Mr. Bradford Wilson. If you're interested in receiving a proposal from him, please step into the carriage."

Joanna looked around at the smiling faces of all the people she loved then to Bradford who had left Snowy's area and was standing on the side of the driveway in front of it. "I am definitely interested." She took the man's hand and climbed in.

Most of Joanna's life was grounded in reality, but a part of her had always dreamed of something like this happening. It was over-the-top romantic and so perfect she almost burst into tears.

The ride to Bradford was short, and she hardly took a breath the whole way. He met the carriage and raised a hand to help her out when she arrived. There was both laughter and love in his eyes. "Too much?"

"It's fucking perfect," she said, knowing the swear would make him laugh and it did.

"Clay helped with the details."

She wiped a happy tear from the corner of her eye. "Really? I would never have guessed."

The next look he gave her was so intense she stopped laughing and swayed. This was the part of the fantasy that mattered—the only part that really mattered. He dropped to one knee and took out a ridiculously ornate ring box. "I didn't want to fall in love. I never imagined myself married with children. I thought I was the type who could never settle down. You drove me insane for so long I was sure we wouldn't work out."

She smiled. "Maybe skip to the part where you changed your mind."

He laughed. "Sorry. I'm nervous."

Her heart melted then. "Don't be. You already know what I'll say. I love you."

He blinked a few times quickly as if fighting back his own tears. "Marry me, Joanna, not because I can promise you that everything will go smoothly, but because I swear to you that no matter what life throws our way I will be there, every day, every time, right at your side. Loving you taught me that I didn't understand love at all before you. You're beautiful, intelligent, and so damn sweet I couldn't help but fall for you. But I'm in this for the long haul. I know now that I will love you just as much when you're full of wrinkles, can't remember shit, and get all crotchety with age."

"Well, who could say no to that? Yes, Bradford, I will marry you." Joanna was laughing when he opened the ring box and revealed a diamond about ten times bigger than she would have imagined choosing, but it was perfect because she guessed he'd taken Clay's advice. She was still laughing when he slipped the ring on her finger.

He stood and they kissed to the sound of applause from all over her farm. "You know the problem with rescues?" he asked.

She looked up at him, so in love she could barely focus on what he was saying. "What?"

"There's always the risk you'll fall in love with one of them and they'll take up the spot that could have gone to others. Snowy and I are kind of a package deal. I'd like to build a barn for him and another horse we rescue to be his pasture buddy."

"We can do that."

"We now own the farms around us. If you decide to expand to working with full-size horses there will be room for that as well."

"Farms? How much land are you talking about?"

"A few hundred acres."

"You're crazy," Joanna said, trying to wrap her head around that. "Were they even for sale?"

"I don't know. You'd have to ask my fairy godfather. He assures me sellers were all well taken care of and happy with the deal he gave them."

"Why would Clay do that for us?"

"He called it a security buffer. When I told him we didn't need that, he called it an early wedding present. I tried to say no, but it made him happy, is probably a tax write-off for him, and it's for a good cause."

"Yes, it is. Wow. Looks like we'll be hiring more help."

"Connor asked if we could employ some of the veteran

families he works with. Especially the families who hit hard times after the loss of a spouse."

Joanna threw her arms around Bradford and broke into happy tears against his chest. "Bradford, I am in this for the long haul too. Get as old, ugly, forgetful, and grumpy as you want. You'll be my old grump."

"Crotchety and Grumpy. You think the sex will still be good?"

Joanna burst out laughing. "If you asked my mother she'd tell you it only gets better with time." At his widened eyes, she added, "Don't actually ask her. She'd tell you way more than you want to know. But she and my father are doing great so that's all that matters."

Bradford looked down the driveway where her parents were standing, arms around each other. "If that's our future it doesn't look bad to me at all." He waved to them.

They waved back.

He said, "Not bad at all."

A SHORT TIME later Joanna stepped away to show her friends her new ring and Bradford stood alone, okay with having a moment to catch his breath. As if by magic, servers with trays of champagne and hor d'oeuvres began to circulate. Tables were being set up with the insane amount of flowers Clay thought necessary for an engagement party. It was unfolding seamlessly and actually looked really nice.

Sophie and Dale walked over to join Bradford. "You did good," Dale said, holding out his hand for Bradford to shake. "Really good."

Bradford shook his hand and smiled. "Thanks, sir. I had help."

Sophie stepped forward and placed her hands on either side of his face. "You deserve all of this and more, Bradford. I'm so proud of you for believing in yourself enough to let it happen."

He gathered her to him and hugged her. They stood there for a long, healing moment. When Bradford stepped back he was a little embarrassed by the display of emotion, but not sorry he'd done it. Ian caught his eye from nearby and smiled with approval.

Lydia and Gerry joined them. "There's my future son-in-law," Gerry said, clapping Bradford on the back.

Lydia gave him a hug so tight Bradford laughed when she stepped back. "I always wanted a son and now I'll have one. We can go to auctions together. Oh, Bradford, the trouble you and I will get into."

Joanna slid in under Bradford's arm. "Neither of you are going without me or Dad. You two softies would bring the whole lot home each time."

"Guilty as charged," Bradford said and kissed her forehead.

"I am so happy for both of you," Sophie said. "And for Clay. He's two for two now."

Bradford sought Clay out in the crowd and nodded his thanks to him. Clay's answering smile meant the message was received. He couldn't have imagined ever choosing to spend time with Clay, but Clay had invited him to meet some of his Gold Star families and it had been a moving experience. There were so many really good people, proud people who wanted to work but needed just a little boost to get back on their feet. Clay might be a bored man entertaining himself by meddling in other people's lives, or he just might be a good man with more money than he knew what to do with, who was always looking for ways to make the world a better place. Either way, he no longer instantly annoyed the shit out of Bradford.

It was a start.

"I wonder who he'll choose to help next?" Bradford asked aloud without meaning to.

Joanna answered, "I suggested Aly and Dylan to him."

Dylan was flirting with one of Joanna's staff and Aly was clear across the party looking as if she were unaware he existed. "Are you sure a gynecologist belongs with a man who still laughs every time he hears the word vagina?"

Joanna snuggled closer and smiled up at him. "I hear opposites attract."

He kissed the tip of her nose. "I've heard the same thing. Stranger things have happened. I always thought I'd be the one to save you."

"You were a tough one at first, but I knew I could win you over."

"Reluctantly rescued."

"Hey, that would make a great title for a book. I just might steal it."

THE END

Not ready to say good-bye to these characters? Sign up for my newsletter via my website ruthcardello.com/newsletter and stay informed about releases.

To get a complete list of all my books to to:
www.Ruthcardello.com

Reluctantly Romanced, The Barrington Billionaires Book 10

About the Author

Ruth Cardello was born the youngest of 11 children in a small city in southern Massachusetts. She spent her young adult years moving as far away as she could from her large extended family. She lived in Boston, Paris, Orlando, New York—then came full circle and moved back to New England. She now happily lives one town over from the one she was born in. For her, family trumped the warmer weather and international scene.

She was an educator for 20 years, the last 11 as a kindergarten teacher. When her school district began cutting jobs, Ruth turned a serious eye toward her second love– writing and has never been happier. When she's not writing, you can find her chasing her children around her small farm, riding her horses, or connecting with her readers online.

Contact Ruth:

Website: RuthCardello.com
Email: Ruthcardello@gmail.com
FaceBook: Author Ruth Cardello
Twitter: @RuthieCardello

Printed in Great Britain
by Amazon

45912899R00145